George Eyre-Todd

Scottish poetry of the seventeenth century

George Eyre-Todd

Scottish poetry of the seventeenth century

ISBN/EAN: 9783337234157

Printed in Europe, USA, Canada, Australia, Japan

Cover: Foto ©Andreas Hilbeck / pixelio.de

More available books at **www.hansebooks.com**

Abbotsford Series

of the

Scottish Poets

Edited by GEORGE EYRE-TODD

SCOTTISH POETRY OF THE
SEVENTEENTH CENTURY

SIR ROBERT AYTOUN
SIR DAVID MURRAY
SIR ROBERT KER
SIR WILLIAM ALEXANDER
WILLIAM DRUMMOND
THE MARQUIS OF MONTROSE
THE SEMPLES OF BELTREES

GLASGOW: WILLIAM HODGE & CO
1895

TO

.

His Grace

The DUKE OF MONTROSE, K.T.,

THIS VOLUME

.

WHICH CONTAINS THE COMPLETE EXTANT POETICAL WORKS

OF

His Heroic Ancestor,

The Most Noble JAMES, MARQUIS OF MONTROSE,

IS

Dedicated.

NOTE.

THERE has hitherto existed no anthology of the
Scottish poetry of the "Stuart Period." Owing to
this circumstance, and to the consequent difficulty
of forming a comprehensive judgment, it has been
usual to consider that period somewhat lightly.
The credit of the productions of the time has
also suffered greatly from the typographical difficulties which have stood in the way of clear
reading. These have been enough, in many cases,
not only to obscure the beauties, but to obliterate
the meaning of the poems. It is hoped that the
present volume, by clearing away these obstructions
and affording means of collective perusal, may help
towards a more popular appreciation of the work
of a neglected century.

CONTENTS.

SCOTTISH POETRY OF THE SEVENTEENTH CENTURY.

IN the year 1603 James VI. passed over Berwick bridge to assume the crown of his English kingdom. It was not, however, till 1707 that the legislative union of England and Scotland was effected. The century between these dates, from the union of the crowns to the union of the parliaments, was in both countries a period of immense significance. The previous century has been marked in British history as the century of Reformation; and with equal justice the seventeenth century may be named the century of Revolution. Nor does this epithet refer merely to the disaster which during that century overtook the throne. In the hundred years which elapsed between the end of the House of Tudor with the death of Elizabeth and the accession of the House of Hanover in the person of George I. a greater revolution than the mere overturn of a

B   V

dynasty was taking place. During the Stuart period, as it has been named, was effected the great passage from ancient to modern times. It was the misfortune rather than the fault of the Stuart kings that they happened to be the rulers at the time of this great change. Their shortcomings, it is true, were many, and they made grievous mistakes, but the period was one of conflict between the old order and the new, between government by the king and government by the people, and by the nature of their office the princes of the time were upon the losing side. No one, at anyrate, can deny that the Stuarts paid dearly for their errors, since one of the race, within the period, suffered on the block, and another was deprived of his throne.

These catastrophes, the execution of Charles I. and the exile of James II., were the great political events which marked the transition effected in the two kingdoms during the seventeenth century. At the same time there are other circumstances, less conspicuous, perhaps, but hardly less significant, which remain tokens of the change. In the Scottish poetry of the period, in particular, a remarkable departure is to be noticed. From the dawn of the century it not only abandoned absolutely all its ancient national fields of inspiration, but actually almost entirely ceased to use the ancient national tongue. The immediate causes of this departure are easily traced.

During the last forty years of the previous century the national mind of Scotland had been convulsed and engrossed by the events of the Reformation. Such a period of struggle is never itself productive of much poetry : song, whether of love or of patriotism, is invariably an after-production. Moreover, the grim new asceticism of the Reformers set its face sternly against what they termed "the profane and unprofitable art of poem-making." By the end of the sixteenth century, owing to these discouragements, the ancient vigorous school of native Scottish poetry had become extinct. The rollicking humour of James V., the biting satire of Lyndsay and Maitland, the quaint love-philosophy of Scot, and the richly coloured allegory of Montgomerie—the entire river of national song, in short, of which these were characteristic features, had ceased to flow. George Buchanan, one of the greatest Scotsmen of his time, it is true, wrote poetry, but he wrote in Latin. The vernacular muse of the country was represented by nothing stronger than such pedantic versifyings as the "Essayes" of James VI., such a sweet but slender rivulet of fancy as Alexander Hume's "Day Aestival," or such

godly imaginings as were set forth in Lady
Culross's " Dream."

Poetry was at this low ebb in Scotland when
the king crossed the Border, and the transference
of the court to London threw the ancient Scots
tongue out of fashion, and brought the southern
idiom into vogue.

At the same time the great era of English
poetry was at its zenith. Marlowe and Spenser
were but lately dead, while Shakespeare was at
the acme of his powers, and was the centre of a
galaxy of dramatic poets the like of which the
world had never seen. It was the time of Ben
Jonson and of Beaumont and Fletcher, of
Massinger, Ford, Webster, and a dozen others.
In the hands of these poets, and of such masters
of prose as Lord Bacon and Sir Philip Sidney,
the English language just then had been wrought
to its highest pitch of dignity, beauty, and
strength. It remains small matter for marvel,
therefore, that the Scottish poets of the new
period were caught by the glamour of the new
fashion, and strove to sing in the tongue of
their English contemporaries.

It can be understood that ability to do this
with sufficient ease and elegance to attract
notice was confined to those few persons whose
education and opportunities had made them
familiar with the speech and literature of the

southern kingdom. Hence it came about that the Scottish poets of note in the seventeenth century were all men of position and rank—a circumstance in itself not without effect upon choice of subject and style of thought.

There must also, it is true, have been a few poets of the people, those nameless, humble singers to whom is owed the folk-song of the time—such ballads as "The Dowie Dens o' Yarrow," "The Bonnie House o' Airlie," and "The Baron o' Brackley." But the ballads of the seventeenth century are singularly few. Barely half-a-dozen of the first rank, indeed, are to be found. They cannot therefore qualify the fact that the body of Scottish poetry of the period followed the southern vogue.

For fifty years this fashion lasted ; the ancient themes, as well as the characteristics and the language, of the Scottish poets of former days were abandoned, and the verse of the north might almost as aptly have been the product of southern pens.

It might have been feared that at such a time the muse of the north, labouring under the double disadvantage of an adopted style and an alien tongue, was in danger of becoming a mere echo of its southern rival. From this abject position it was saved by a few great names, not all of the first rank in poesie,

indeed, but all entitled to an honourable place
and esteem beside those of the English singers
of their day. Even in that great English era,
from the time of Spenser to that of Dryden,
which included the transcendent names of
Shakespeare and Milton, the Scottish poetry
cannot be passed by which contains the stren-
uous passion of Montrose, the sense and dignity
of the Earl of Stirling, and the wit, grace, and
harmony of Drummond of Hawthornden.

When these poets ceased to sing a great
silence fell upon the muse of the country. The
latest of the group, Drummond and Montrose,
died within eighteen months of the execution of
Charles I. After that event Scotland descended
to one of the most troubled periods of her
history. First came the civil wars of Charles
II., followed by the irksome domination of
Cromwell. Next, after the death of the Pro-
tector, hardly had Monk marched south with his
Coldstream levies and inaugurated the Restoration, when the fierce and bloody struggles began
between Episcopacy and the Covenanters. These
struggles were ended in 1688 by the Revolution
and the flight of James II.; but the Revolution
in turn gave rise to the equally fierce conflicts
of Jacobites and Whigs, which lasted over the
end of the century. During the whole period
the country was torn by the dissensions of nobles

and churchmen, prelates and presbyters ; and men had enough to think about to keep their heads on their shoulders, without turning attention to a leisurely art like the writing of poetry.

In England circumstances were somewhat different ; there was room for Milton to sit apart in his blindness and compose " Paradise Lost"; and in the precarious sunshine of the Merry Monarch's court there was warmth enough to quicken the song of the Cavalier poets. But in Scotland there was storm and night, and notwithstanding a flash here and there, as in the case of the Semples, from the smouldering embers of the ancient popular muse, Scottish poetry, during the second half of the seventeenth century, must be held to have reached its nadir.*

When, in 1707, the head centre of national dissension and party strife was removed by the transference of the Scottish parliament to London, and the country emerged from its long period of discord and conflict to a new era of prosperity and enterprise, its entire social system had undergone a change. The feudalism of the Middle Ages in church and state had passed

* In support of this statement it will be enough to refer he reader to the bald Covenanting ballads of the period and to compositions like those of Dr. Pennycuik, author of the " Description of Tweeddale."

finally away, and had given place to the con-
stitutional order of modern days.   Very soon
the new era declared itself in the national poetry.
Allan Ramsay struck the note boldly again upon
Scottish character and Scottish manners, and,
reviving interest in the ancient ballads of the
country, gave the first signal for the great
Romantic movement of northern Europe, which
culminated in Goethe, Balzac, and Scott.

SIR ROBERT AYTOUN.

SIR ROBERT AYTOUN.

As the first Scottish poet of note who elected to write in Shakespeare's English, Sir Robert Aytoun remains a figure of peculiar interest in the literary history of Scotland. In several aspects, indeed, his career may be noted as typical. He began life, like so many young Scotsmen of his time, as an obscure, wandering scholar-adventurer, yet he became the trusted servant and friend of two kings and two queens. And though he filled a post of high consideration at a critical period in history, his best title to remembrance lies in the verses which he wrote as a relaxation from more serious duties. He represents, in short, a characteristic figure of that age—the courtier among poets who was no less a poet among courtiers.

Aytoun's descent has been traced from the Norman house of De Vescy, barons of Sprouston in Northumberland, through one Gilbert de Vescy, who in the fourteenth century received the lands of Eiton or Aytoun, in Berwickshire, from Robert the Bruce. The poet, a younger son, was born in his father's castle of Kinaldie, near St. Andrews, in 1570. He graduated at St. Andrews University in 1584, and on his father's death in 1590, receiving his slender patrimony, he went abroad, studying civil law at the University of Paris, and exercising his leisure with the writing of Latin poetry. In 1603, however, occurred the accession of James VI. to the throne of England, and, seeing in that event an opportunity not to be lost, Aytoun hastened home and addressed to the king a congratulatory Latin poem of considerable length and no small tact. This performance had the good fortune to attract the royal notice, and James, eager to attach men of literary talent to his person, invited the author to court, and installed him for the nonce one of the Grooms of the Privy Chamber.

Aytoun throve at court. When James acknowledged the authorship of the "Apology for the Oath of Allegiance," the poet was one of the two envoys sent to convey the royal dedication to Rudolph II., Emperor of Germany, and the other princes of Europe. This mission he appears to have fulfilled to the king's satisfaction, for on his return Aytoun was knighted at Rycot in Oxfordshire, and about the same time was appointed both Gentleman of the Bedchamber to James himself and Private Secretary to the queen. In 1619 he received a grant of £500 per annum for thirty-one years out of certain moneys accruing to the royal exchequer. This in the following July was converted into a life pension, on account of "services rendered to the king and his late consort."

Along with Bacon, in 1623, Aytoun became a candidate for the provostship of Eton. His chief motive for seeking this somewhat lucrative post was, it appears, to benefit the children of the former provost, Thomas Murray, who had been his early friend. In support of his candidature he addressed a poetical epistle to the king, but although James was understood to favour his views, the post finally fell to Sir Henry Wotton, himself no inconsiderable poet, as well as a scholar of repute.

On the death of James in 1625 Aytoun was continued in his office by Charles I., and was appointed Secretary to Queen Henrietta Maria. These posts apparently enabled him to exercise considerable private influence at court. His name, at anyrate, is found mixed up with a case in which certain claims to a patent for camleting silk were disputed between two London tradesmen and two Pages of the Bedchamber. Evidence, moreover, is not wanting which proves that he stood well in the esteem of his royal mistress. In 1636 the queen appointed him Master of St. Katherine's Hospital, a sinecure in her own gift, worth £200 a year.*

---

* St. Katherine's Hospital, which was founded in 1148 by Matilda, wife of the usurper Stephen, occupied, in Aytoun's time, a site which is now covered by St. Katherine's Dock. Its patronage was vested in the queen-consort, and this so strictly as to give rise, some fifty years ago, to a singular dilemma. In the early years of Queen Victoria's reign the mastership became vacant. Curiously enough, Her Majesty was then found disqualified to make the new appointment, and the power of nomination was accordingly exercised by Adelaide, the Queen Dowager.

In the royal household Aytoun successively filled the further posts of Master of Requests and Master of Ceremonies; and Charles finally showed his appreciation of the services and sagacity of his attendant by appointing him a Privy Councillor.

The old courtier-poet died as he had lived, within the royal precincts, and happily passed away before the clouds of misfortune drew to their darkest round the head of his royal master. Aytoun breathed his last in the palace of Whitehall in February 1637-38, in his 69th year, and the splendid monument erected over his grave in Westminster Abbey by his nephew and heir, Sir John Aytoun, still bears witness to his honours.

Aytoun's character appears to have been one of singular tact and worldly prudence, combined with modest dignity and great kindliness of heart. With all his good fortune he seems to have escaped the fate of most men in his position. Dempster says of him that "he conducted himself with such moderation and prudence that when he obtained high honours in the palace, all held that he deserved greater." At the same time the old courtier did not forget his kin. With true Scottish family feeling, he procured for his nephew a small situation in the Household, from which he afterwards became Gentleman Usher of the Black Rod. Aubrey, in his *Lives of Eminent Men*, states that Aytoun "was acquainted with all the wits of his time in England." The general esteem in which he was held, however, is perhaps best testified by Ben Jonson's assurance to Drum-

mond at Hawthornden that "Sir Robert Aytoun
loved him dearly."

In a prefatory note the poet's nephew has left on
record that Aytoun "did not affect the name of a
poet, having neither published in print nor kept copies
of anything he writ, either in Latin or English." Of
his Latin poems a MS. was at one time preserved in
the Advocates' Library at Edinburgh; but this has
disappeared, and all of his Latin poems now known
are owed to Scot of Scotstarvet's *Delitiæ Poetarum
Scotorum*. His English poems have been preserved
in two MSS. One, a thin folio of forty-three pages,
containing corrections by Sir John Aytoun, is among
the Additional MSS. in the British Museum. The
other, "The Poems of that Worthy Gentleman, Sir
Robert Aytoun, Knight," was in the possession of
the poet's editor, the Rev. Charles Rogers. Several
of the pieces were included in the collections of
Watson and Pinkerton, and the English poems were
edited together by Dr. Rogers in 1844. A more
complete edition, including the surviving Latin
poems, was printed privately by the same editor at
London in 1871, the memoir and English poems
being reproduced in the first volume of *Transactions
of the Royal Historical Society*.

As a poet, Aytoun appears entitled to higher consideration than he has yet received. Notwithstanding
Dryden's statement, quoted by Aubrey, that he considered Aytoun's verse "some of the best of that
age," this typical Jacobean singer has suffered no
little neglect. Nothing that he wrote, indeed, can

be held to rival the lyric perfection of verses like
Ben Jonson's "Drink to me only." It is true, as
well, that the range of his muse is limited. The
actual quantity of his verse is not large, and what
there is of it mostly concerns "the boy that bears,"
as Aytoun himself puts it, "the stately style of Love."
Love, however, as every reader of the verse of that
age is aware, was almost exclusively the subject of
the lyric poetry of the time; and the other lyric
poets of the day were even more limited in the
quantity of their compositions. Letting pass, therefore, the first great flight of Shakespearean singers,
Aytoun appears entitled upon his actual merits to
rank among the best, as he was among the earliest,
of those graceful dalliers with a courtly muse who
have become known as the Cavalier poets.

His claim to be the first of the Scottish poets to
write in English rests on the fact that his "Diophantus
and Charidora" was produced before the accession
of James VI. to Elizabeth's throne in 1603. The
fashion of writing in English, thus set, was immediately followed by Sir William Alexander, who produced his early work, the *Aurora*, in 1604, and by
Drummond, who composed his "Tears on the Death
of Mæliades" in 1613. "Diophantus and Charidora"
is a long and conventional production, though here
and there it has a characteristic line, as when
Diophantus swears "by the Stygian stanks of Hell,"
or declares of his mistress that

> She is mine by lot of love,
> Though luck in love I want.

In one of its verses, curiously, the poet anticipates Tennyson :—

> For if of all mishaps
> This be the first of all,
> To have been highly happy once,
> And from that height to fall.

It is by his later and shorter pieces, however, that Aytoun should be best remembered. In these he has expressed, better perhaps than any other, the modest dignity of unfortunate but self-respecting love. The ring of genuine feeling in his verse is not to be mistaken. It is this which has prevented the Jacobean courtier-poet from becoming old-fashioned, while his touch of gentle stateliness has endued him with a delicate and perennial charm.

C   V

THE LOVER'S REMONSTRANCE.

DEAR, why do you say you love,
When indeed you careless prove?
Reason better can digest
Earnest hate, than love in rest.

Wherefore do your smiling eyes
Help your tongue to make sweet lies?
Leave to statesman tricks of state;
Love doth politicians hate.

You perchance presume to find
Love of some chameleon kind;
But be not deceived, my fair,
Love will not be fed on air.

Love's a glutton of his food;
Surfeits make his stomach good:
Love whose diet grows precise
Sick from some consumption dies.

Then, dear love, let me obtain
That which may true love maintain;
Or, if kind you cannot prove,
Prove true—say you cannot love.

THE EXERCISE OF AFFECTION.

THERE is no worldly pleasure here below
  Which by experience doth not folly prove;
But, among all the follies that I know,
  The sweetest folly in the world is love.

But not that passion which, by fools' consent,
  Above the reason bears imperious sway,
Making their lifetime a perpetual Lent,
  As if a man were born to fast and pray.

No! that is not the humour I approve,
  As either yielding pleasure or promotion;
I like a mild and lukewarm zeal in love,
  Although I do not like it in devotion.

For it hath no coherence with my creed
  To think that lovers die as they pretend.
If all that say they die had died indeed,
  Sure long ere now the world had had an end.

Besides, we need not love but if we please;
  No destiny can force man's disposition;
And how can any die of that disease
  Whereof himself may be his own physician?

But some seem so distracted of their wits
    That I would think it but a venial sin
To take some of those innocents that sit
    In Bedlam out, and put some lovers in.

Yet some men, rather than incur the slander
    Of true apostates, will false martyrs prove ;
But I am neither Iphis nor Leander,
    I'll neither drown nor hang myself for love.

Methinks a wise man's actions should be such
    As always yield to reason's best advice.
Now, for to love too little or too much
    Are both extremes, and all extremes are vice.

Yet have I been a lover by report,
    Yea, I have died for love, as others do ;
But, praised be God, it was in such a sort
    That I revived within an hour or two.

Thus have I lived, thus have I loved till now,
    And found no reason to repent me yet ;
And whosoever otherwise will do
    His courage is as little as his wit.

SONG.

WHAT means this strangeness now of late,
  Since time doth truth approve?
This distance may consist with state,
  It cannot stand with love.

'Tis either cunning or distrust
  That doth such ways allow.
The first is base, the last's unjust;
  Let neither blemish you.

If you intend to draw me on,
  You over-act your part,
And if you mind to send me gone,
  You need not half this art.

Speak but the word, or do but cast
  A look which seems to frown,
I'll give you all the love that's past;
  The rest shall be my own.

And such a fair and equal way
  On both sides, none can blame,
Since every one is bound to play
  The fairest of his game.

TO A VARIABLE MISTRESS.

WHY did I wrong my judgement so
As to affect where I did know
 There was no hold for to be taken?
That which her heart thirsts after most,
If once of it her hope can boast,
 Straight by her folly is forsaken.

Thus, while I still pursue in vain,
Methinks I turn a child again,
 And of my shadow am a-chasing:
For all her favours are to me
Like apparitions which I see,
 Yet ne'er come near th' embracing.

Oft have I wished that there had been
Some almanac whereby to 've seen
 When love with her had been in season.
But I perceive there is no art
Can find the epact of the heart
 That loves by chance, and not by reason.

Yet will I not for this despair;
For time her humour may prepare
 To love him who is now neglected:
For what unto my constancy
Is now denied, one day may be
 From her inconstancy expected.

TO AN INCONSTANT MISTRESS..

I LOVED thee once, I'll love no more,
　Thine be the grief, as is the blame;
Thou art not what thou wast before,
　　What reason should I be the same?
　　He that can love unloved again
　　Hath better store of love than brain;
　　God send me love my debts to pay,
　　While unthrifts fool their love away!

Nothing could have my love o'erthrown
　If thou hadst still continued mine;
Nay, if thou hadst remained thine own
　　I might perchance have yet been thine.
　　But thou thy freedom did recall
　　That it thou might elsewhere enthrall,
　　And then how could I but disdain
　　A captive's captive to remain?

When new desires had conquered thee,
　And changed the object of thy will,
It had been lethargy in me,
　　Not constancy, to love thee still:
　　Yea, it had been a sin to go
　　And prostitute affection so,
　　Since we are taught no prayers to say
　　To such as must to others pray.

Yet do thou glory in thy choice,
Thy choice of his good fortune boast;
I'll neither grieve nor yet rejoice
To see him gain what I have lost.
The height of my disdain shall be
To laugh at him, to blush for thee;
To love thee still, but go no more
A-begging at a beggar's door.

THE AUTHOR'S ANSWER.

Written at the King's Command.

THOU that loved once, now lov'st no more,
  For fear to show more love than brain;
With heresy unhatched before,
  Apostasy thou dost maintain.
    Can he have either brain or love
    That doth inconstancy approve?
    A choice well made no change admits,
    And changes argue after-wits.

Say that she had not been the same,
  Shouldst thou therefore another be?
What thou in her as vice did blame,
  Can that take virtue's name in thee?
    No, thou in this her captive was,
    And made thee ready by her glass;
    Example led revenge astray,
    When true love should have kept the way.

True love hath no reflecting end;
  The object good sets all at rest;
And noble breasts will freely lend
  Without expecting interest.

'Tis merchant love, 'tis trade for gain,
To barter love for love again;
'Tis usury, nay, worse than this,
For self-idolatry it is.

Then let her choice be what it will,
　Let constancy be thy revenge;
If thou retribute good for ill,
　Both grief and shame shall check her change.
　　Thus mayst thou laugh, when thou shalt see
　　Remorse reclaim her home to thee;
　　And where thou beg'st of her before,
　　She now sits begging at thy door.

THE FORSAKEN MISTRESS.*

I DO confess thou'rt smooth and fair,
  And I might have gone near to love thee
Had I not found the slightest prayer
  That lips could speak had power to move thee.
    But I can let thee now alone
    As worthy to be loved by none.

I do confess thou'rt sweet, yet find
  Thee such an unthrift of thy sweets,
Thy favours are but like the wind
  Which kisseth everything it meets;
    And since thou canst love more than one
    Thou'rt worthy to be loved by none.

* The authorship of this poem cannot with certainty be
attributed to Aytoun. It does not appear in Sir John Aytoun's
MS., and in Watson's Collection of Scots Poems it is printed
with no author's name attached. Dr. Rogers, in including it,
urged the similarity to Aytoun's sentiment and style. It appeared
set to music in Playford's "Select Ayres" under the title of a
"Song to his Forsaken Mistress." Burns paid it the compliment
of attempting to "improve the simplicity of the sentiments by
giving them a Scottish dress"; but it cannot be said that the
version of the Ayrshire bard at all equals the original.

The morning rose that untouched stands,
    Armed with her briers, how sweet she smells!
But plucked, and strained through ruder hands,
    Her sweet no longer with her dwells;
        But scent and beauty both are gone,
        And leaves fall from her one by one.

Such fate, ere long, will thee betide,
    When thou hast handled been awhile,
Like fair flowers to be thrown aside,
    And thou shalt sigh when I shall smile
        To see thy love to every one
        Hath brought thee to be loved by none.

UNRECOMPENSED DEVOTION.

My Fair's unkind, and I have spent my pains,
And purchased nothing but undue disdains.
Oh, had she been as kind as I was true,
What praise to her, what joy to me'd been due!
But to my grief and her disgrace I find
That fair ones too much loved prove seldom kind.
What then? Shall loving less be my revenge?
Oh no! I wrong my judgement if I change.
The dice are cast, and, let her loathe or love,
I may unhappy, not inconstant prove;
For it is quite impossible for me
To love her less, as more in love to be.

SONNET

Left in a Lady's Mirror.

To view thy beauty well, if thou be wise,
  Come not to gaze upon this glass of thine;
  But come and look upon these eyes of mine,
Where thou shalt see thy true resemblance twice.
Or, if thou think'st that thou profan'st thine eyes,
  When on my wretched eyes they deign to shine,
  Look on my heart, wherein, as in a shrine,
The lovely picture of thy beauty lies.
Or, if thy harmless modesty think shame
  To gaze upon the horrors of my heart,
Come read these lines, and, reading, see in them
  The trophies of thy beauty, and my smart.
Or, if to none of these thou'lt deign to come,
Weep eyes, break heart, and then my verse be
    dumb.

ON A LADY THAT WAS PAINTED.

PAMPHILIA hath a number of good arts,
Which commendation to her worth imparts;
But, above all, in one she doth excel—
That she can paint incomparably well.
And yet so modest that, if praised for this,
She'll swear she does not know what painting is,
But straight will blush with such a portrait grace
That one would think vermilion dyed her face.
One of her pictures I have ofttimes seen,
And would have sworn that it herself had been;
And when I bade her it on me bestow,
I swear I heard the picture's self say No.
What! think you this a prodigy?   'Tis none—
The painter and the picture both were one.

ON TOBACCO.

FORSAKEN of all comforts but these two,
  My faggot and my pipe, I sit and muse
  On all my crosses, and almost accuse
The Heavens for dealing with me as they do.
Then Hope steps in, and with a smiling brow
  Such cheerful expectations doth infuse
  As make me think erelong I cannot choose
But be some grandee, whatsoe'er I'm now.

But having spent my pipe, I then perceive
That hopes and dreams are cousins—both deceive.
  Then make I this conclusion in my mind,
'Tis all one thing—both tend into one scope—
To live upon tobacco and on hope:
  The one's but smoke, the other is but wind.

SIR DAVID MURRAY.

SIR DAVID MURRAY.

AMONG the various Scotsmen at the English court of
James VI. who occupied their leisure, and perhaps
helped their fortunes, by the occasional exercise of
an elegant poetic pen, Sir David Murray of Gorthy
cannot be passed over. By his contemporaries he
appears to have been held in high esteem, as much
for his poetic taste as for his courtly connection,
and his sonnets remain typical examples of the poetic
vein fashionable among the court gallants of his time.

A younger son of Robert Murray of Abercairney
by a daughter of the house of Tullibardine, his circumstances were those of the Scotsman so familiar
in the English epigram of the period—the youth of
good family but slender purse, who looked to a place
at court as his natural provision for life. Unlike
many of his less fortunate fellows, however, he not
only attained his desire in this respect, but gained
the trust and affection of his royal master to an un-
common degree. He was at first attached to the
person of Prince Henry in the capacity of First
Gentleman of the Bedchamber; and when in 1610
the prince's household was definitely fixed, Murray

became Groom of the Stole and Gentleman of the
Robes. According to a contemporary he was regarded by the heir to the throne as the most reliable
of his attendants—"the onely man in whom he put
choise trust." He appears to have been in equal
favour with the king, for when, probably like most
other court gallants, he found his affairs in difficulties,
he received from James a free gift, first of £2000 and
then of £5200, expressly stated to be for the payment
of his debts. These gifts occurred in 1613 and 1615
respectively, and in 1630 they were capped by a grant
from King Charles of the estate of Gorthy. He
seems, however, to have remained unmarried, and he
died without succession.*

Murray's longest poem is "The Tragicall Death of
Sophonisba," published at London in 1611. It forms
one of the evidences of the revival of taste for Italian
models then going on, the subject having been a
favourite one with Italian poets of the previous century. As a work upon its own merits, Murray's poem
can hardly be said to deserve immortality. Apart
from its startling anachronisms and obtrusive conceits, its chief fault is a want of action and energy.
It flows along in soliloquies of little interest, never
rising to true passion nor melting to real pathos.
Much of it indeed is mere measured prose.

Printed with "Sophonisba" was a collection of
poems entitled "Coelia," consisting chiefly of sonnets
addressed to the poet's mistress. It is upon some

* Douglas's *Baronage of Scotland*, p. 102.

of these that Murray must depend for his poetic fame. They are not, it is true, marked by any striking originality, but among the faults common to the poetry of the time—a constant tendency to conceits and conventional phrases—they display a certain richness of colouring and air of ancient courtliness which render them, like some stately old garden of their time, still pleasant to wander through.

The volume of 1611 was reprinted for the Bannatyne Club at Edinburgh in 1823.

A QUESTION.

AND is it true, dear, that you are unkind?
　　Shall I believe, sweet saint, that you are so?
　　I fear you are; but stay, O stay, my mind!
Too soon to credit that that breeds my woe.
　　Yet whither shall my resolutions go?
To think you are, or not, unkind, I must.
　　Th' effect says Aye, and yet my fancy No,
Being loth such undeserved harm to trust.
My passions thus such operations breed
　　In my divided soul, that I cannot
Conceive you are that which you are indeed,
　　Imperious love doth so control my thought.
Unhappy I that did such love embrace!
Unconstant you that hates such love, alas!

HIS MISTRESS.

BRIGHT angel's face, the paradise of love—
  High stately throne where majesty doth shine—
  Beauty's idea, sweetness' sweetened shrine—
Clear heavens, wherein proud Phœbus' dazzlers
  move—
Fair pearly rolls that stain the ivory white,
  Environed with coral-dyed walls—
  Sweet-nectared breath, more soft than Zephyr's
  gales—
Heart-reiving tongue, whose speech still breeds
  delight—
Smooth cheeks of rose and lilies interlaced—
  Art-scorning nose, in framing which, no doubt,
  Nature of her whole skill played bankerout,
When it in midst of such perfections placed—
Gold-glittering tresses, and souls-wounding locks—
Only proud ears, more deaf than flinty rocks!

ADIEU!

ADIEU, sweet Cœlia! for I must depart
 And leave thy sight, and with thy sight all joy,
 Convoyed with care, attended with annoy,
A vagabonding wretch from part to part.
Only, dear Cœlia, grant me so much grace
 As to vouchsafe this heart befraught with sorrow
 T' attend upon thy shadow even and morrow,
Whose wonted pleasure was to view thy face.

And if sometimes thou solitar remain,
 And for thy dearest dear a sigh lets slide,
 This poor attender, sitting by thy side,
Shall be thy echo, to reply 't again.
Then farewell, Cœlia! for I must away,
And to attend thee my poor heart shall stay.

LOVE'S IDEA.

DAYS, hours, and nights thy presence may detain,
  But neither day nor hour nor night shall not
Bar thy sweet beauty from mine eyes unseen,
  Since so divinely printed in my thought.
  That skilful Greek that Love's idea wrought,
And limned it so exactly to the eye,
  When beauty's rarest patterns he had sought,
With this thy portrait could not matched be.
Though on a table he—most skilful he—
  In rarest colours rarest parts presented,
So on a heart, if one may match a tree,
  Though skill-less, I thy rarer shape have painted.
Not by Love's self Love's beauty formed he;
But by thyself thyself art formed in me.

LOVE'S ACCOMPT.

PONDER thy cares, and sum them all in one,
  Get the account of all thy heart's disease,
  Reckon the torments do thy mind displease,
Write up each sigh, each plaint, each tear, each groan,
Remember on thy grief conceived by day,
  And call to mind thy night's disturbed rest,
  Think on those visions did thy soul molest
While as thy wearied corpse a-sleeping lay ;
And when all those thou hast enrolled aright
  Into the 'count-book of thy daily care,
  Extract them truly, then present the sight
  With them, of flinty Cœlia the fair,
That she may see if yet more ill remains
For to be paid to her unjust disdains.

SIR ROBERT KER.

SIR ROBERT KER,

EARL OF ANCRAM.

AMONG poets whose fame lives by reason of a single composition must be included the first Earl of Ancram. One sonnet, " In Praise of a Solitary Life," is all of his original work now known to be extant.

In Douglas's " Peerage of Scotland," II., 136, a full account is furnished of Sir Robert Ker's ancestry. He was descended from a long line of Border chieftains, most conspicuous of whom probably was his great-grandfather Sir Andrew Ker of Fernihirst, one of the most striking figures on the marches in the reigns of James IV. and James V. Himself the representative of the house of Fernihirst, the poet would appear to have inherited the traditions of his stormy race in a career of vicissitude and romantic adventure.

To begin with, in 1590, when he was no more than twelve years of age, in the course of an outstanding feud with the rival house of Cessford, his father was assassinated. The perpetrator of the deed was Sir Robert Ker, afterwards first Earl of Roxburgh ; and the heir of Ancram by rule of vendetta inherited the blood-debt. This however, in 1606, at the instance

E   V of the Council and the earnest entreaty of the king, he consented to forego, and so closed the feud. Again, later in life, when he had risen to a high position at court, his influence appears to have excited the jealousy of the unscrupulous Duke of Buckingham. In consequence, one Charles Maxwell of Terregles fixed a quarrel upon the poet, and forced him to a duel. This was fought at Newmarket in February, 1620, apparently on horseback, and resulted in the death of Maxwell. A verdict of manslaughter was given against Ker, and he received the regular sentence of burning in the hand. The sentence, however, was commuted to banishment, and after an exile of six months he received the king's pardon.

Ker held the appointment of Groom of the Bed-chamber, first to the young Prince Henry and afterwards to Prince Charles, accompanying the royal household to England in 1603 in that capacity. About 1605 he received the honour of knighthood. In the following years, besides holding many high offices at Whitehall, he was employed on several missions to Scotland, and on at least one abroad, to the court of Bohemia. His most romantic expedition, however, was undertaken in company with Prince Charles. When the heir to the throne, following the romantic example of his great-grandfather, James V., went over, incognito, to Spain to adventure a suit with the Infanta, he was accompanied by Sir Robert Ker. It is unfortunate, perhaps, that the experiences of the royal party upon that expedition are not better known.

From first to last Charles appears to have held his
early attendant in high esteem : at the coronation in
Scotland in 1633 he raised him to the peerage as
Earl of Ancram, and he also conferred upon him
several valuable grants and concessions, culmin-
ating in a pension of £2000 a year. Ker on his
side seems to have fully justified the confidence
placed in him. Throughout all the troubles of the
time he remained steadily faithful to the royal house,
and upon the execution of the king he retired to
Amsterdam, where, in 1654, after some years of great
privation, he died at the age of 76. So deep, indeed,
were the distresses entailed upon him by his loyalty
that after his death his body was arrested for debt,
and it was only upon the intercession of Cromwell
that the burial was allowed to take place.

Ker's eldest son, William, having married Anne,
heiress of an elder branch of the family and Countess
of Lothian in her own right, was created Earl of
Lothian in 1631, and from him the present Marquis
of Lothian is directly descended. With this son, who
had espoused the cause of Parliament and the Covenant, as well as with others of his family, and with
some of the most distinguished men of the day, the
exiled earl kept up a correspondence. This correspondence, known as "the Lothian Papers," was
published in 1875, with a memoir and portrait, for
the Bannatyne Club, and it throws considerable light
on the events of the time.

Among the acquaintance of his happier days the
old courtier appears to have counted John Donne and

Drummond of Hawthornden ; and Sage, in his life of
the last-named poet, records a quaint anecdote of
Drummond peeping into a room in a London tavern,
and discovering Ben Jonson, Michael Drayton, Sir
William Alexander, and Sir Robert Ker laughing and
chatting together.

The sonnet " In Praise of a Solitary Life " was
enclosed in a letter to Drummond, dated December
1, 1644, which is included in the Correspondence.
The author states that he sends the sonnet because
his friend " was so kind to the last," from which it
may be gathered that the earl was the writer of other
compositions.   The only other verse of his which has
survived, however, is a set of paraphrases in metre of
eleven of the Psalms.   These have been preserved in
the Drummond MSS., and are printed in the appendix
to the Correspondence.   They are dated 1624, and
were written, it is recorded, to suit certain Dutch and
French measures to which Ker had heard the Psalms
sung when he was abroad.

As a man, the Earl of Ancram appears to have
filled a high position with modesty, ability, and entire
trustworthiness, and when misfortunes came upon him
he bore them with firmness and piety.

As a poet, there is naturally not much to be
said regarding him.   His sonnet can be read at a
glance, and conveys its own impression.   Certainly
its author's criticism upon it cannot be accepted
as final.   " The date of this starved rhyme," he
wrote, " and the place, was the very Bed-chamber,
where I could not sleep."

It is, however, rather as a member of a group which would be incomplete without him that he is entitled to regard—that group of accomplished gentlemen, scholars, poets, and courtiers, whom James VI. carried in his train across the Border, and who, at a period when the feat was unusually difficult, enabled the Court to establish itself with respect amid the brilliance of English genius.

IN PRAISE OF A SOLITARY LIFE.

WEET solitary life! lovely, dumb joy,
    That need'st no warnings how to grow
        more wise
By other men's mishaps, nor the annoy
  Which from sore wrongs done to one's self doth
      rise—
The morning's second mansion, truth's first friend,
  Never acquainted with the world's vain broils;
When the whole day to our own use we spend,
  And our dear time no fierce ambition spoils!
Most happy state, that never tak'st revenge
  For injuries received, nor dost fear
The court's great earthquake, the grieved truth of
    change,
  Nor none of falsehood's savoury lies dost hear;
Nor know'st hope's sweet disease, that charms our
    sense,
Nor its sad cure—dear-bought experience!

FIRST PSALM.

THE man is blest whom no lewd counsel can
　　Entice to turn from the right path aside,
Nor sit with the ill-natured, scornful man,
　　Nor in the way of sinners will abide;
But on God's law doth study day and night,
And takes great care how he may keep it right.

He shall be like a goodly tree that grows
　　Near to a river, where no summer's heat
Nor winter, with his eager frosts and snows,
　　Doth scorch the leaves, nor yet the branches beat,
Nor yet the owner's greedy hope deceive,
But yields him as much fruit as he can crave.

With the ungodly it shall not be so,
　　Because they do neglect the Lord's command.
Look how a whirling wind the dust doth blow
　　Or how the chaff from out the corn is fanned:
So shall the Lord them utterly deface,
That where they have been none can shew the place.

And when the Judge shall in the clouds appear
To give true judgment upon good and bad,
The godly may look up with joyful cheer,
But the ungodly fearfully and sad ;
For He that all our secret thoughts doth view
Will give each one according to his due.*

* In the paraphrase both of this Psalm and of that which here
succeeds, the poet professedly follows the famous Latin version of
George Buchanan.

PSALM CXXX.

DEEP sunk in floods of grief,
  Unto the Lord I prayed
That he would send relief,
  And thus my sad heart said:

Lord, hear the sighs and groans
  That I before Thee pour,
Listen unto my moans
  And help me at this hour.

If, like a judge severe,
  To punish Thou be bent,
No flesh can be so clear
  As to prove innocent.

But merciful Thou art,
  And from all passion free;
But, Lord, it is our part
  With fear to trust in Thee.

Thy word, mine only hope,
  Sustains my wavering mind,
And in that faithful prop
  All confidence I find.   .

No watchman of the night
   More longeth for the day
Than I do for the light
   Which Thy grace doth display.

Then trust the Lord all ye
   That do Him fear and know,
For it is only He
   That helps the weak and low.

SIR WILLIAM ALEXANDER.

SIR WILLIAM ALEXANDER,

EARL OF STIRLING.

Of all the figures typical of the times of Elizabeth and James VI. in England, probably the most characteristic, and certainly the most picturesque, was the gentleman-adventurer. To say nothing of the Drakes and Frobishers who sought fortune on the high seas and on the Spanish Main, there were men of another class, like Edmund Spenser, Sir Philip Sidney, and Sir Walter Raleigh, equally ready to compete for honour with the pen or with the sword—to shine at court, to plant colonies abroad, to take hard blows on the battlefield, or to indite poetry or history as occasion offered. Among Scotsmen of this type the most conspicuous figure of the time remains that of the first Earl of Stirling. In the matter of reputation and enterprises, no less than in vicissitudes of fortune, a close parallel might be drawn between this nobleman and Sir Walter Raleigh.

The family of Alexander of Menstrie,* which reached its highest position in the person of the poet-earl, traced its descent from Somerled, Lord of

---

* " Menstrie "—appropriately enough, " the minstrel."

the Isles in the time of Malcolm IV. Its immediate ancestor was John, Lord of the Isles, who married Margaret, daughter of Robert II. The grandsons of John of the Isles were Angus, founder of the family of M'Alister of Loup, and Alexander, who obtained from the Argyle family a grant of the lands of Menstrie, near Stirling, and settled there. Sixth in descent from this first holder of the estate was William Alexander, the poet.

Born in 1580, and probably educated first at the neighbouring grammar school of Stirling, he is known to have attended Glasgow University, and after leaving college to have travelled on the continent as tutor to Archibald, the young seventh Earl of Argyle. During these travels he is supposed to have written the series of songs, sonnets, madrigals, sestinets, and elegies, published in 1604 under the title of "Aurora." Different views have been entertained as to the lady to whom these effusions were addressed; but from sonnet 104 and the final song it appears all but certain that the subject of the series was the lady who became his wife—Janet, daughter and heiress of Sir William Erskine.

In 1603, having returned to Scotland, he published his "Tragedy of Darius." This he reprinted in 1604 with a second poetic drama, the "Tragedy of Crœsus"; and these, with the "Alexandræan Tragedy," published in 1605, and "Julius Cæsar" in 1607, made up the quatrain which in the last-named year attracted universal praise when issued under the title of *Monarchic Tragedies.*

Meanwhile Alexander was not unknown at court,
and in 1604, having followed King James to London,
he definitely attracted the royal attention and favour
by the publication of his "Paræncsis to Prince
Henry." This procured him an appointment as one
of the gentlemen of the Prince's privy chamber—the
first step on the ladder of his adventurous public
fortunes. He held this post till the Prince's death in
1612, an event which, as in duty bound, he enlarged
upon in an "Elegy on the Death of Prince Henry."

In the following year James, who appears to have
had a particular regard for Alexander, calling him
his philosophical poet, appointed him one of the
gentlemen ushers to Prince Charles. The royal
favour was still further shown in 1614 in an
appointment as Master of Requests, and by the
king's conferring upon the poet the honour of
knighthood. In that year Alexander ended his
poetical career for the time by the publication of
"Doomsday, or the Great Day of the Lord's Judgment," a ponderous performance in four "Hours"
or books. It is true that twenty-three years later,
in 1637, under the title of *Recreations with the
Muses*, he republished most of his poems in collected
form, with "Doomsday" enlarged to twelve Hours,
and with the addition of the first book of a new
heroic poem entitled "Jonathan." But from 1614
his career must be regarded rather as that of the
courtier, statesman, and man of affairs than as that
of the poet.

In 1611, probably with a view to further the

F   V

colonization of Ireland, begun in Elizabeth's time, the king had founded the order of Baronets of Ulster; and in 1621 in furtherance of a similar policy for Nova Scotia, James conferred upon Sir William Alexander probably the largest concession ever granted to a subject. This was no less than a free gift by charter of the whole of Canada, including Nova Scotia and Newfoundland. At the same time it was ordered that persons of approved position, upon purchase of five thousand acres of the land of the colony, for which the price was set at £150, should be created hereditary Baronets of Nova Scotia. For four years the enterprise rested at this point; but in 1625 the grant was confirmed by Charles I., whereupon Sir William, in support of the undertaking, issued a pamphlet entitled "An Encouragement to Colonies," and the creation of the new baronetcies began.

In 1626 Alexander was made Secretary of State for Scotland, and other tokens of the royal confidence rapidly followed. He was made Keeper of the Signet in 1627, and a Commissioner of Exchequer in 1628, and, having been raised to the peerage as Viscount Stirling and Baron Alexander of Tullibody in 1630, he was appointed one of the Extraordinary Lords of Session in 1631. Finally, upon the Scottish coronation of Charles in 1633, he was created Earl of Stirling and Viscount Canada.* To these titles was added that of Earl of Dovan in 1639.

---

* Upon that occasion Charles created one marquis, ten earls, two viscounts, and eight barons.

In February of the following year, 1640, while in London prosecuting the business of his various offices, the earl died, having seen the first beginnings of the storm which was rising to overwhelm the throne, but being spared a knowledge of the tragic end which awaited his royal master.*

No career of the time, excepting, perhaps, that of Sir Walter Raleigh or of Charles I. himself, presents a picture of such brilliant endeavour combined with such uniform misfortune as the career of the Earl of Stirling. His reputation as a man suffered very seriously from the circumstances of his time. Much has been said of his venality in the matter of the Canadian concession; but his impeachment on this score must now be looked on chiefly as a result of popular rancour. Similar concessions, if none so large, were about that time made to several men of enterprise who undertook to found colonies abroad, and curiously enough, within recent years the identical method has once more been resorted to in the concessions to the various companies engaged in

* Lockhart in his life of Scott, chap. ii., furnishes an interesting footnote. On Sir Walter's copy of *Recreations with the Muses*, his biographer, it appears, found the following MS. note :—" Sir William Alexander, sixth Baron of Menstrie and first Earl of Stirling, the friend of Drummond of Hawthornden and Ben Jonson, died in 1640. His eldest son, William, Viscount Canada, died before his father, leaving one son and three daughters by his wife, Lady Margaret Douglas, eldest daughter of William, first Marquis of Douglas. Margaret, the second of these daughters, married Sir Robert Sinclair of Longformacus in the Merse, to whom she bore two daughters, Anne and Jean. Jean Sinclair, the younger daughter, married Sir John Swinton of Swinton ; and Jean Swinton, her eldest daughter, was the grandmother of the proprietor of this volume."

founding the British empire in Africa. It does not
appear that Alexander profited to any undue extent
by the Nova Scotia baronets' payments for grants
of land. In return for these he had probably to
bear the entire cost of the two expeditions which
were sent out to the colony, as well as the charges
of administration and of establishing the settlement
at Port Royal. He seems, indeed, rather to have
been out of pocket by the transaction, for when it
was found that by Charles First's ill-advised treaties
with the French not only the newly captured
Quebec, but the British colonists' headquarters at
Port Royal, as well as the lesser British settle-
ments, had to be abandoned, the king, in name
of losses, made Alexander a gift of £10,000.

The loss of their lands, however, enraged the new-
made baronets, and this, with the failure of the
colony, which appears to have been mostly a Scottish
one, rendered Sir William most unpopular at home.
Other circumstances increased this feeling. He had
the misfortune to be Secretary of State during the
period of Charles's attempt to introduce the English
form of church government and church service into
Scotland, and he had in consequence upon this
account also, to bear the brunt of popular antipathy.
Everything he did was, in popular fashion, turned to
matter of personal obloquy. He was known to have
received a patent monopoly for thirty-one years of
printing King James' version of the Psalms in metre
—the version which the people, in the endeavour to
introduce the English liturgy, were enjoined to use.

He was also, as Governor of Canada, licensed to issue a small coin called a "turner," regarding which the popular grievance was that the real value was considerably less than the nominal—a peculiarity not then considered just, though it is the characteristic of the whole modern British coinage except gold. Accordingly when, in 1632, to support his various dignities, Alexander built himself a handsome town mansion on the castle hill of Stirling, and inserted above the doorway his family motto—" Per mare, per terras "—that motto was parodied as " Per metre, per turners." A report was also industriously spread that the grant of £10,000 made to Alexander by the king as a return for his Canadian losses, was in reality a bribe to betray the colony to the French ; and it can be understood that the statesman's hardship was made none the less by the fact that the grant was never paid.*

Whatever were the merits of the case, it is probably safe to say that when in July, 1637, Jenny Geddes threw her stool at the Dean of Edinburgh's head in St. Giles' Cathedral, there was no name more execrated by the lips of the furious populace than that of the unfortunate Secretary.

As a matter of fact, Lord Stirling appears to have been a heavy loser by his public enterprises. Upon his death his affairs were found to be insolvent, and

---

* The editor of Alexander's works states that in 1660 a petition was presented to Charles II. by the Ladies Mary and Jane Alexander for payment of this money. The petition was graciously received, and handed to the Lord Chamberlain to report upon, but apparently received no further attention.

the mansion which had been the object of so much
spiteful reference passed into the possession of the
Argyle family.

Nor did the Earl's sacrifices and ill-fortune end with
loss of means. His eldest son, a young man of great
promise, who had married a daughter of the first
Marquis of Douglas, and had gone out as deputy
lieutenant to manage the affairs of Nova Scotia, lost
his health there, and died two years before his father.
Lord Stirling's infant grandson, who succeeded to the
honours of the earldom, enjoyed them only for a few
months ; and on the death of the fifth earl, a
descendant of the poet's younger son, Henry, in
1739, the title became dormant.

Two unsuccessful attempts have been made to
revive the honours, and upon the later occasion the
consequent trial, like the great Douglas Cause and
the Breadalbane Case, remains one of the famous
law-cases of the peerage.

The fullest account of the Earl of Stirling's life is
that prefixed to the Secretary's own *Register of Royal
Letters*, published for the Grampian Club in 1885 by
the Rev. Charles Rogers, LL.D. From this account,
as well as from the substance of the Earl's own
writings, it is to be gathered that, as the latest
editor of his poetry expresses it, far from cherishing
the tyrannical and time-serving principles popularly
attributed to him, " few men of his time held such
manly and independent theories of the duties of
sovereignty, or dared to express them so openly as
he ; and few men have shewn themselves possessed of

more practical ideas as to the method and working of governments, shewing how they were to rule, and how in their own turn they were to be ruled and watched over, than the poet, philosopher, and statesman of Menstrie."

Following his own collection of his works, the *Recreations with the Muses*, published in 1637, the earl's poems were twice reprinted in part—once, on Addison's recommendation, by A. Johnston, in 1720, and again, in Chalmers' heavy collection of British poets, in 1810. The first and only complete edition was printed by Maurice Ogle & Co. in three volumes at Glasgow, in 1870. This edition, however, does not include two poems, "The Comparison" and "The Solsequium," printed in Ramsay's *Evergreen*, which have been attributed to the earl.

Besides his recognized poetry, Alexander, in 1613, published a completion of the third part of Sir Philip Sidney's *Arcadia*, which has been included in the fourth and subsequent editions of that work. There are also substantial grounds for believing that he was himself author of the greater part of the version of Psalms in metre attributed to King James.

But it is with the Earl's acknowledged and secular poetry that we are here chiefly concerned.

It is true that the greater part of his longer poems, notwithstanding the praise of Addison, cannot but be considered as tedious by the modern reader. They possess, however, certain claims to high credit which must not be overlooked. Of his "Doomsday," or Day of Judgement, it may be urged that a work of such

huge moral scope could only be rendered readable by
genius of the very highest order. Nevertheless, the
varied knowledge, the power of reflection, and the
vigour of intellect which it displays have been pointed
out as entitling their possessor to no mean esteem,
and, a somewhat significant circumstance, the work
is said to have furnished Milton with the suggestion
of "Paradise Lost." Similar exception has been taken
to the "Monarchic Tragedies." Founded upon the
Greek model, these are philosophical poems rather
than dramas intended for performance. They exhibit
almost no action, the events with which they deal
being always narrated as occurring off the stage.
They present, however, a series of noble soliloquys
and reflections, and almost every page sparkles with
some brilliant and sage aphorism. The scene between
Brutus and Portia in "Julius Cæsar" may be cited as
an almost unsurpassed picture of an ideal conjugal
union, and the speech of Olympias before execution
in the "Alexandræan Tragedy" might almost have
been written by Christopher Marlowe. For their
shrewdness, dignity, and sense, no less than for their
frequent passages of poetic beauty, the "Monarchic
Tragedies" attracted universal admiration in their
time, and were praised by poets of repute like
Drummond, Drayton, and Daniel; while it has been
shown that even Shakespeare did not disdain to
borrow suggestions from them.

Alexander's best poem, however, is his "Parænesis,"
or exhortation, to Prince Henry, afterwards readdressed
to the prince who became Charles II. This contains

perhaps the finest extant directions for kingly rule.
Full of wise lessons derived from the successes
and mistakes of the rulers of the past, the poem
anticipates the highest modern ideas of kingship.
Alexander, for instance, has anticipated Tennyson in
teaching that the throne should be broad-based upon
the people's will—a very daring doctrine for the
seventeenth century ; and he has gone further than
Tennyson in indicating the means whereby this
foundation may be secured :—

> Kings should excell all those whom they command
> In all the parts which do command respect, &c.

Here, more, perhaps than in any other of his works,
shines the poet-statesman's wonderful tact when
treading upon delicate ground. What, for example
could be more courtly and yet sensible, under the
peculiar circumstances, in reference to a monarch like
James VI., than the advice to Prince Henry to adopt
as a kingly model his sire—not, however, in trivial
things, but only in those "matchless virtues which all
minds admire." It says much for the poet's power
of wisely gauging character that in this Parænesis he
gave warning against exactly those mistakes which
within the half-century cost Charles I. his head and
James II. his throne.

"Aurora," though Alexander did not republish it,
remains its author's most charming poem. There
appears to have been a vogue, just then, of sonnets in
series, owing probably to the revived interest of the
time in Petrarch and the Italian poets. Shakespeare's

sonnets are an instance of this vogue; Alexander's
"Aurora" is another. The "Aurora" it is true,
contains various forms of verse, but of the whole the
sonnets remain by far the finest part. The theme of
the series is the perennial one of love, and the sonnets
by themselves present a very complete epitome of a
lover's varying mood's and fortunes.

This poem by itself would entitle Alexander to a
high place among the courtly singers of his time,
whom it matches upon their own field of love. When
to this are added the graver qualities of his other
works, no doubt can remain of his claim, not only to
stand next to Drummond among the Scottish poets of
the century, but to rank among the foremost of the
second flight of English Jacobean singers.

An undue neglect has hitherto been Alexander's
fortune at the hands of literary appraisers. For this
the great extent of his writings is largely to blame,
hiding the grains of gold in an earthen bed. But
the insight, wisdom, and independent spirit, apart
from the frequent beauties of his work, must always
make even his longest poems worth perusal, and
among the monuments of his time and of Scotland a
niche of high honour of his own must remain to the
Earl of Stirling as distinctively the poet-counsellor
of kings.

SONNETS AND SONGS FROM "AURORA."

UNSPOKEN LOVE.

NCE to debate my cause whilst I drew near,
　My staggering tongue against me did con-
　　spire.
And whilst it should have charged it did retire—
A certain sign of love that was sincere.
I saw her heavenly virtues shine so clear
　That I was forced for to conceal my fire,
　And with respects even bridling my desire.
More than my life I held her honour dear,
And though I burned with all the flames of love,
　Yet, frozen with a reverent kind of fears,
　I durst not pour my passions in her ears,
Lest so I might the hope I had remove.
Thus love marred love, desire desire restrained;
Of mind to move a world, I dumb remained.

INCONSTANT FORTUNE.

Sestinet.

HARD is my fortune, stormy is my state,
And as inconstant as the waving sea,
Whose course doth still depend upon the winds :
For lo, my life, in danger every hour,
And though even at the point for to be lost,
Can find no comfort but a flying show.

And yet I take such pleasure in this show
That still I stand contented with my state,
Although that others think me to be lost,
And whilst I swim amidst a dangerous sea,
'Twixt fear and hope, are looking for the hour
When my last breath shall glide amongst the winds.

Lo, to the seaman beaten with the winds
Sometimes the heavens a smiling face will show,
So that to rest himself he finds some hour ;
But nought, ah me ! can ever calm my state,
Who, with my tears as I would make a sea,
Am, flying Scylla, in Charybdis lost.

The pilot that was likely to be lost,
When he hath 'scaped the furor of the winds
Doth straight forget the dangers of the sea ;

But I, unhappy I, can never show
No kind of token of a quiet state,
And am tormented still from hour to hour.

O shall I never see that happy hour
When I, whose hopes once utterly were lost,
May find a means to re-erect my state,
And leave for to breathe forth such dolorous winds,
Whilst I myself in constancy do show
A rock against the waves amidst the sea.

As many waters make in end a sea,
As many minutes make in end an hour,
And still what went before th' effect doth show,
So all the labours that I long have lost,
As one that was but wrestling with the winds,
May once in end concur to bless my state.

And once my storm-stead state saved from the sea,
In spite of adverse winds, may in one hour,
Pay all my labours lost, at least in show.

AN ARGUMENT.

I SWEAR, Aurora, by thy starry eyes,
  And by those golden locks whose lock none slips,
  And by the coral of thy rosy lips,
And by the naked snows which beauty dyes;
I swear by all the jewels of thy mind,
  Whose like yet never worldly treasure bought,
  Thy solid judgment and thy generous thought,
Which in this darkened age have clearly shined;
I swear by those and by my spotless love,
  And by my secret, yet most fervent fires,
  That I have never nursed but chaste desires,
And such as modesty might well approve.
Then, since I love those virtuous parts in thee,
Shouldst thou not love this virtuous mind in me?

BASE AND NOBLE THRALDOM.

THE thoughts of those I cannot but disprove
  Who, basely lost, their thraldom must bemoan;
  I scorn to yield myself to such a one
Whose birth and virtue is not worth my love.
No, since it is my fortune to be thrall,
  I must be fettered with a golden band;
And if I die, I'll die by Hector's hand,
So may the victor's fame excuse my fall;
And if by any means I must be blind,
  Then it shall be by gazing on the sun.
  Oft by those means the greatest have been won,
Who must like best of such a generous mind.
At least by this I have allowed of fame
Much honour if I win, if lose, no shame.

THE COST OF PRIDE.

O, IF thou knewest how thou thyself dost harm,
  And dost prejudge thy bliss and spoil my rest,
  Then thou wouldst melt the ice out of thy breast,
And thy relenting heart would kindly warm.
O, if thy pride did not our joys control,
  What world of loving wonders shouldst thou see!
  For if I saw thee once transformed in me,
Then in thy bosom I would pour my soul.
Then all thy thoughts should in my visage shine,
  And if that ought mischanced thou shouldst not
      moan,
  Nor bear the burthen of thy griefs alone.
No, I would have my share in what were thine,
And whilst we thus should make our sorrows one,
This happy harmony would make them none.

THE PAIN OF LOVING.

When I behold that face for which I pined
  And did myself so long in vain annoy,
  My tongue not able to unfold my joy,
A wond'ring silence only shows my mind.
But when again thou dost extend thy rigour,
  And wilt not deign to grace me with thy 'sight,
  Thou kill'st my comfort, and so spoil'st my might,
That scarce my corps retains the vital vigour.
Thy presence thus a great contentment brings,
  And is my soul's inestimable treasure;
  But O, I drown in th' ocean of displeasure
When I in absence think upon those things.
Thus would to God that I had seen thee never,
Or would to God that I might see thee ever!

THE SOVEREIGN GOOD.

O NOW I think, and do not think amiss,
   That th' old philosophers were all but fools,
   Who used such curious questions in their schools,
Yet could not apprehend the highest bliss.
Lo, I have learned in th' academe of love
   A maxim which they never understood;
   To love and be beloved, this is the good
Which for most sovereign all the world will prove.
That which delights us most must be our treasure,
   And to what greater joy can one aspire
   Than to possess all that he doth desire
Whilst two united souls do melt in pleasure?
This is the greatest good can be invented,
That is so great it cannot be augmented.

ON HEARING OTHERS' MISTRESSES PRAISED.

WHEN whiles I hear some gallants to give forth
  That those whom they adore are only fair,
  With whom they think none other can compare,
The beauty of beauty and the height of worth ;
Then jealousy doth all my joys control,
  For O, I think, who can accomplished be—
  There is no sun but one—save only she
Whom I have made the idol of my soul ?
And this suspicion wounds my better parts ;
  I rage to have a rival in my light,
  And yet would rage far more if any might
Give her their eyes and yet hold back their hearts.
Too great affection doth those passions move,
I may not trust my shadow with my love.

OF CONSTANCY.

FEAR not, my fair, that ever any chance
  So shake the resolutions of my mind
  That, like Demophon, changing with the wind,
I thy fame's rent not labour to enhance.
The ring which thou in sign of favour gave
  Shall from fine gold transform itself in glass;
  The diamond, which then so solid was,
Soft like the wax, each image shall receive;
First shall each river turn unto the spring.
  The tallest oak stand trembling like a reed,
  Harts in the air, whales on the mountains feed,
And foul confusions seize on everything,
Before that I begin to change in aught,
Or on another but bestow one thought.

THE BURNING FIRE OF LOVE.

WHEN as the sun doth drink up all the streams,
  And with a fervent heat the flowers doth kill,
  The shadow of a wood or of a hill
Doth serve us for a targe against his beams.
But ah, those eyes that burn me with desire,
  And seek to parch the substance of my soul,
  The ardour of their rays for to control
I wot not where myself for to retire.
'Twixt them and me, to have procured some ease,
  I interposed the seas, woods, hills, and rivers,
  And yet am of those never-emptied quivers
The object still, and burn, be where I please.
But of the cause I need not for to doubt—
Within my breast I bear the fire about.

OF AN OLD SAYING.

OFT have I heard, which now I must deny,
　That nought can last if that it be extreme;
　Times daily change, and we likewise in them;
Things out of sight do straight forgotten die.
There is nothing more vehement than love,
　And yet I burn, and burn still with one flame;
　Times oft have changed, yet I remain the same;
Nought from my mind her image can remove.
The greatness of my love aspires to ruth;
　Time vows to crown my constancy in th' end,
　And absence doth my fancies but extend.
Thus I perceive the poet spake the truth,
That who to see strange countries were inclined
Might change the air, but never change the mind.

PARADOX.

I HOPE, I fear, resolved, and yet I doubt,
  I'm cold as ice, and yet I burn as fire;
  I wot not what, and yet I much desire,
And trembling too, am desperately stout.
Though melancholious wonders I devise,
  And compass much, yet nothing can embrace,
  And walk o'er all, yet stand still in one place,
And, bound on th' earth, do soar above the skies.
I beg for life, and yet I bray for death,
  And have a mighty courage, yet despair.
  I ever muse, yet am without all care,
And shout aloud, yet never strain my breath.
I change as oft as any wind can do,
Yet for all this am ever constant too.

A REASON FOR SUFFERING.

THE most refreshing waters come from rocks,
  Some bitter roots oft send forth dainty flowers,
  The growing greens are cherishèd with showers,
And pleasant stems spring from deformèd stocks.
The hardest hills do feed the fairest flocks,
  All greatest sweets were sugared first with sours,
  The headless course of uncontrollèd hours
To all difficulties a way unlocks.
I hope to have a heaven within thine arms,
  And quiet calms when all these storms are past,
  Which, coming unexpected at the last,
May bury in oblivion bygone harms.
To suffer first, to sorrow, sigh, and smart,
Endears the conquest of a cruel heart.

AGAINST DELAY.

Ah, thou, my love, wilt lose thyself at last,
  Who can to match thyself with none agree.
  Thou ow'st thy father nephews, and to me
A recompence for all my passions past.
Ah, why shouldst thou thy beauty's treasure waste,
  Which will begin for to decay, I see?
  Erst, Daphne did become a barren tree
Because she was not half so wise as chaste ;
And all the fairest things do soonest fade,
  Which O, I fear, thou with repentance try ;
  The roses blasted are, the lilies die,
And all do languish in the summer's shade.
Yet will I grieve to see those flowers fall down
Which for my temples should have framed a crown.

DEFECT OF LOVE.

SMALL comfort might my banished hopes recall,
　　When whiles my dainty fair I sighing see,
　　If I could think that one were shed for me
It were a guerdon great enough for all;
Or would she let one tear of pity fall,
　　That seemed dismissed from a remorseful eye,
　　I should content myself ungrieved to die,
And nothing might my constancy appall.
The only sound of that sweet word of love,
　　Pressed 'twixt those lips that do my doom contain,
　　Were I embarked might bring me back again
From death to life, and make me breathe and move.
Strange cruelty, that never can afford
So much as once one sigh, one tear, one word.

THE DEBT OF LOVE.

I WOT not which to challenge for my death,
  Of those thy beauties, that my ruin seeks—
  The pure white fingers, or the dainty cheeks,
The golden tresses, or the nectared breath.
Ah, they be all too guilty of my fall;
  All wounded me, though I their glory raised,
  Although I grant they need not to be praised—
It may suffice they be Aurora's all.
Yet for all this, O most ungrateful woman,
  Thou shalt not scape the scourge of just disdain,
  I gave thee gifts thou shouldst have given again:
It's shame to be in thy inferiors common.
I gave all what I held most dear to thee,
Yet to this hour thou never guerdoned me.

A PETITION.

WHILST careless swimming in thy beauty seas
   I wond'ring was at that bewitching grace,
   Thou painted pity on a cruel face,
And angled so my judgment by mine eyes;
But now, begun to triumph in my scorn,
   When I cannot retire my steps again,
   Thou armst thine eyes with envy and disdain
To murther my abortive hopes half born.
Whilst, like to end this long continued strife,
   My paleness shows I perish in despair,
   Thou, loth to lose one that esteems thee fair,
With some sweet word or look prolongst my life,
And so each day in doubt redact'st my state.
Dear, do not so, once either love or hate?

BEAUTY AND WORTH.

To yield to those I cannot but disdain
  Whose face doth but entangle foolish hearts.
  It is the beauty of the better parts
With which I mind my fancies for to chain.
Those that have nought wherewith men's minds to
      gain
  But only curled locks and wanton looks,
  Are but like fleeting baits that have no hooks,
Which may well take, but cannot well retain.
He that began to yield to th' outward grace,
  And then the treasures of the mind doth prove,
  He who, as 'twere, was with the mask in love,
What doth he think when as he sees the face?
No doubt, being limed by th' outward colours so,
That inward worth would never let him go.

AWAKE!

AWAKE, my Muse, and leave to dream of loves!
　Shake off soft fancy's chains! I must be free.
　I'll perch no more upon the myrtle tree,
Nor glide through th' air with beauty's sacred doves;
But with love's stately bird I'll leave my nest,
　And try my sight against Apollo's rays;
　Then, if that aught my venturous course dismays,
Upon the olive's boughs I'll light and rest.
I'll tune my accents to a trumpet now,
　And seek the laurel in another field.
　Thus I that once, as beauty means did yield,
Did divers garments on my thoughts bestow,
Like Icarus, I fear, unwisely bold,
Am purposed others' passions now t' unfold.

LOVE RESOLVED.

FAREWELL, sweet fancies, and once dear delights,
  The treasures of my life, which made me prove
That unaccomplished joy that charmed the sprites,
  And whilst by it I only seemed to move,
Did hold my ravished soul, big with desire,
That, tasting those, to greater did aspire.

Farewell, free thraldom, freedom that was thrall
  While as I led a solitary life,
Yet never less alone, whilst, armed for all,
  My thoughts were busied with an endless strife,
For then, not having bound myself to any,
I, being bound to none, was bound to many.

Great god, that tam'st the gods' old-witted child,
  Whose temples breasts, whose altars are men's
    hearts,
From my heart's fort thy legions are exiled,
  And Hymen's torch hath burned out all thy darts;
Since I in end have bound myself to one,
That by this means I may be bound to none.

Thou dainty goddess with the soft white skin,
  To whom so many off'rings daily smoke,
Were beauty's process yet for to begin,
  That sentence I would labour to revoke,
Which on Mount Ida, as thy smiles did charm,
The Phrygian shepherd gave to his own harm.

And if the question were referred to me,
  On whom I would bestow the ball of gold,
I fear me Venus should be last of three;
  For with the Thunderer's sister I would hold,
Whose honest flames, pent in a lawful bounds,
No fear disturbs, nor yet no shame confounds.

I mind to speak no more of beauty's dove.
  The peacock is the bird whose fame I'll raise:
Not that I Argos need to watch my love,
  But so his mistress Juno for to praise:
And if I wish his eyes, then it shall be
That I with many eyes my love may see.

Then farewell crossing joys and joyful crosses!
  Most bitter sweets, and yet most sugared sours!
Most hurtful gains, yet most commodious losses,
  That made my years to flee away like hours,
And spent the springtime of mine age in vain,
Which now my summer must redeem again.

O welcome easy yoke! sweet bondage, come!
  I seek not from thy toils for to be shielded,
But I am well content to be o'ercome,
  Since that I must command when I have yielded.
Then here I quit both Cupid and his mother,
And do resign myself t' obtain another.

A PARÆNESIS TO PRINCE HENRY.

Lo here, brave youth, as zeal and duty move,
  I labour, though in vain, to find some gift
Both worthy of thy place, and of my love;
  But whilst myself above myself I lift,
And would the best of my inventions prove,
  I stand to study what should be my drift;
Yet this the greatest approbation brings,
Still to a prince to speak of princely things.

When those of the first age that erst did live
  In shadowy woods, or in a humid cave,
And taking that which th' earth not forced did give,
  Would only pay what nature's need did crave;
Then beasts of breath such numbers did deprive,
  That, following Amphion, they did deserts leave,
Who with sweet sounds did lead them by the ears,
Where mutual force might banish common fears.

Then building walls, they barbarous rites disdained,
  The sweetness of society to find;
And to attain what unity maintained,
  As peace, religion, and a virtuous mind,

H   V

That so they might have restless humours reined,
    They straight with laws their liberty confined,
And of the better sort the best preferred,
To chastise them against the laws that erred.

I wot not if proud minds who first aspired
    O'er many realms to make themselves a right;
Or if the world's disorders so required,
    That then had put Astræa to the flight;
Or else if some whose virtues were admired,
    And eminent in all the people's sight,
Did move peace-lovers first to rear a throne,
And give the keys of life and death to one.

That dignity, when first it did begin,
    Did grace each province and each little town.
Forth, when she first doth from Benlomond run,
    Is poor of waters, naked of renown,
But Carron, Allan, Teith, and Dovan in,
    Doth grow the greater still, the further down,
Till that, abounding both in power and fame,
She long doth strive to give the sea her name.

Even so those sovereignties which once were small,
    Still swallowing up the nearest neighbouring state,
With a deluge of men did realms appall,
    And thus th' Egyptian Pharoahs first grew great;
Thus did th' Assyrians make so many thrall,
    Thus reared the Romans their imperial seat,
And thus all those great states to work have gone,
Whose limits and the world's were all but one.

But I'll not plunge in such a stormy deep,
  Which hath no bottom, nor can have no shore,
But in the dust will let those ashes sleep,
  Which, clothed with purple, once th' earth did
      adore ;
Of them scarce now a monument we keep,
  Who, thundering terror, curbed the world before;
Their states, which by a number's ruin stood,
Were founded, and confounded both, with blood.

If I would call antiquity to mind,
  I for an endless task might then prepare ;
But what ? ambition, that was ever blind,
  Did get with toil that which was kept with care,
And those great states 'gainst which the world repined,
  Had falls as famous as their risings rare,
And in all ages it was ever seen,
What virtue raised, by vice hath ruined been.

Yet registers of memorable things
  Would help, great Prince, to make thy judgment
      sound,
Which to the eye a perfect mirror brings,
  Where all should glass themselves who would be
      crowned.
Read these rare parts that acted were by kings,
  The strains heroic, and the end renowned ;
Which, whilst thou in thy cabinet dost sit,
Are worthy to bewitch thy growing wit.

And do not, do not thou the means omit,
   Times matched with times, what they beget to spy,
Since history may lead thee unto it—
   A pillar whereupon good sp'rits rely,
Of time the table, and the nurse of wit,
   The square of reason, and the mind's clear eye,
Which leads the curious reader through huge harms,
Who stands secure whilst looking on alarms.

Nor is it good o'er brave men's lives to wander,
   As one who at each corner stands amazed.
No, study like some one thyself to render,
   Who to the height of glory hath been raised;
So Scipio, Cyrus, Cæsar, Alexander,   [praised.
   And that great Prince choosed him whom Homer
Or make, as which is recent, and best known,
Thy father's life a pattern for thine own.

Yet, marking great men's lives, this much impairs
   The profit which that benefit imparts,
While as, transported with preposterous cares,
   To imitate but superficial parts.
Some for themselves frame of their fancies snares,
   And shew what folly doth o'er-sway their hearts':
For counterfeited things do stains embrace,
And all that is affected, hath no grace.

Of outward things who, shallow wits, take hold,
   Do shew by that they can no higher win.
So, to resemble Hercules of old,
   Mark Antony would bear the lion's skin;

A brave Athenian's son, as some have told,
  Would such a course, though to his scorn, begin,
And bent, to seem look like his father dead,
  Would make himself to lisp, and bow his head.

They who would rightly follow such as those,
  Must of the better parts apply the powers,
As the industrious bee advis'dly goes,
  To seize upon the best, shun baser flowers.
So, where thou dost the greatest worth disclose,
  To compass that, be prodigal of hours.
Seek not to seem, but be. Who be, seem too.
Do carelessly, and yet have care to do.

Thou to resemble thy renowned sire,   [things,
  Must not, though some there were, mark trivial
But matchless virtues, which all minds admire,
  Whose treasure to his realms great comfort brings.
That to attain, thou race of kings! aspire,
  Which for thy fame may furnish airy wings;
And like to eaglets thus thou prov'st thy kind,
When both like him in body and in mind.

Ah, be not those most miserable souls,
  Their judgments to refine who never strive,
Nor will not look upon the learned scrolls,
  Which without practice do experience give;
But, whilst base sloth each better care controls,
  Are dead in ignorance, entombed alive?
'Twixt beasts and such the difference is but small—
They use not reason, beasts have none at all.

O heavenly treasure which the best sort loves,
  Life of the soul, reformer of the will,
Clear light which from the mind each cloud removes,
  Pure spring of virtue, physic for each ill,
Which in prosperity a bridle proves,
  And in adversity a pillar still!
Of thee the more men get, the more they crave,
And think, the more they get, the less they have.

But if that knowledge be required of all,
  What should they do this treasure to obtain,
Whom in a throne time travels to install,
  Where they by it of all things must ordain?
If it make them, who by their birth were thrall,
  As little kings, whilst o'er themselves they reign,
Then it must make, when it hath throughly graced them,
Kings more than kings, and like to him who placed
    them.

This is a grief which all the world bemoans,
  When those lack judgment who are born to judge,
And, like to painted tombs or gilded stones,
  To troubled souls cannot afford refuge.
Kings are their kingdoms' hearts, which, tainted once,
  The bodies straight corrupt in which they lodge;
And those by whose example many fall
Are guilty of the murder of them all.

The means which best make majesty to stand
  Are laws observed, whilst practice doth direct:
The crown the head, the sceptre decks the hand,
  But only knowledge doth the thoughts erect.

Kings should excel all them whom they command,
　In all the parts which do procure respect;
And this a way to what they would, prepares,
Not only as thought good, but as known theirs.

Seek not due reverence only to procure
　With shows of sovereignty and guards oft lewd;
So Nero did, yet could not so assure
　The hated diadem, with blood embrued:
Nor as the Persian kings, who lived obscure,
　And of their subjects rarely would be viewed;
So one of them was secretly o'er-thrown,
And in his place the murderer reigned unknown.

No, only goodness doth beget regard,
　And equity doth greatest glory win;
To plague for vice, and virtue to reward,
　What they intend, that, bravely, to begin:
This is to sovereignty a powerful guard,
　And makes a prince's praise o'er all come in:
Whose life, his subjects law, cleared by his deeds,
More than Justinian's toils, good order breeds.

All those who o'er unbaptized nations reigned,
　By barbarous customs sought to foster fear,
And with a thousand tyrannies constrained
　All them whom they subdued their yoke to bear;
But those whom great Jehovah hath ordained
　Above the Christians lawful thrones to rear,
Must seek by worth to be obeyed for love,
So, having reigned below, to reign above.

O happy Henry, who art highly born,
  Yet beautifi'st thy birth with signs of worth,
And, though a child, all childish toys dost scorn,
  To shew the world thy virtues budding forth,
Which may by time this glorious isle adorn,
  And bring eternal trophies to the north,
While as thou dost thy father's forces lead,
And art the hand, whileas he is the head.

Thou, like that gallant thunder-bolt of war,
  Third Edward's son, who was so much renowned,
Shalt shine in valour as the morning star,
  And plenish with thy praise the peopled round.
But like to his, let nought thy fortune mar,
  Who in his father's time did die uncrowned!
Long live thy sire, so all the world desires,
But longer thou, so Nature's course requires.

And, though time once thee by thy birth-right owes
  Those sacred honours which men most esteem,
Yet flatter not thyself with those fair shows
  Which often-times are not such as they seem,
Whose burdenous weight, the bearer but o'er-throws,
  That could before of no such danger deem:
Then if not, armed in time, thou make thee strong,
Thou dost thyself and many a thousand wrong.

Since thou must manage such a mighty state,
  Which hath no borders but the seas and skies,
Then, even as he who justly was called great
  Did, prodigal of pains where fame might rise,

With both the parts of worth in worth grow great,
    As learned as valiant, and as stout as wise,
So now let Aristotle lay the ground,
    Whereon thou after may thy greatness found.

For if, transported with a base repose,
    Thou did'st, as thou dost not, misspend thy prime,
O what a fair occasion would'st thou lose,
    Which after would thee grieve, though out of time !
To virtuous courses now thy thoughts dispose,
    While fancies are not glued with pleasure's lime.
Those who their youth to suchlike pains engage,
Do gain great ease unto their perfect age.

Magnanimous now, with heroic parts,
    Shew to the world what thou dost aim to be,
The more to print in all the people's hearts
    That which thou would'st they should expect of
That so, preoccupied with such deserts,   [thee ;
    They after may applaud the heavens' decree
When that day comes, which, if it comes too soon,
Then thou and all this isle would be undone.

And otherwise what trouble should'st thou find,
    If first not seized of all thy subjects love,
To ply all humours till thy worth have shined,
    That even most malcontents must it approve ;
For else a number would suspend their mind,
    As doubting what thou afterwards might'st prove,
And when a state's affections thus are cold,
Of that advantage foreigners take hold.

I grant in this thy fortune to be good,
　That art t' inherit such a glorious crown—
As one descended from that sacred blood,
　Which oft hath filled the world with true renown,
The which still on the top of glory stood,
　And not so much as once seemed to look down—
For who thy branches to remembrance brings,
Count what he list, he cannot count but kings.

And pardon me, for I must pause a while,
　And at a thing of right to be admired.　　[isle,
Since those from whom thou cam'st reigned in this
　Lo, now of years even thousands are expired,
Yet none could there them thrall, nor thence exile,
　Nor ever failed the line so much desired :
The hundred and seventh parent living free,
A never-conquered crown may leave to thee.

Nor hath this only happened as by chance ;
　Of alterations then there had been some.
But that brave race which still did worth enhance,
　Would so presage the thing that was to come,
That this united Isle should once advance,
　And, by the Lion led, all realms o'er-come.
For if it kept a little free before,
Now, having much, no doubt it must do more.

And though our nations long, I must confess,
　Did roughly woo before that they could wed,
That but endears the union we possess,
　Whom Neptune both combines within one bed.

All ancient injuries this doth redress,
    And buries that which many a battle bred :
Brave discords reconciled, if wrath expire,
Do breed the greatest love, and most entire.

Of England's Mary had it been the chance
    To make King Philip father of a son,
The Spaniard's high designs so to advance,
    All Albion's beauties had been quite o'er-run.
Or yet if Scotland's Mary had heired France,
    Our bondage then had by degrees begun :
Of which, if that a stranger hold a part,
To take the other that would means impart.

Thus from two dangers we were twice preserved
    When as we seemed without recovery lost,
As from their freedom those who freely swerved,
    And suffered strangers of our bounds to boast.
Yet were we for this happy time reserved,
    And, but to hold it dear, a little crossed,
That of the Stewarts the illustrious race
Might, like their minds, a monarchy embrace.

Of that blest progeny, the wellknown worth
    Hath of the people a conceit procured,
That from the race it never can go forth,
    But, long hereditary, is well assured.
Thus, son of that great monarch of the north,
    They to obey are happily inured,
O'er whom thou art expected once to reign.
To have good ancestors one much doth gain.

He who by tyranny his throne doth rear,
  And dispossess another of his right,
Whose panting heart dare never trust his care,
  Since still made odious in the people's sight,
Whilst he both hath, and gives, great cause of fear,
  Is, spoiling all, at last spoiled of the light,
And those who are descended of his blood,
Ere that they be believed, must long be good.

Yet though we see it is an easy thing
  For such a one his state still to maintain,
Who, by his birthright born to be a king,
  Doth with the country's love the crown obtain,
The same doth many to confusion bring,
  Whilst, for that cause, they care not how they reign.
O never throne established was so sure,
Whose fall a vicious prince might not procure.

Thus do a number to destruction run,
  And so did Tarquin once abuse his place,
Who for the filthy life he had begun,
  Was barred from Rome, and ruined all his race;
So he whose father of no king was son,
  Was father to no king, but, in disgrace
From Sicily banished by the people's hate,
Did die at Corinth in an abject state.

And as that monarch merits endless praise
  Who by his virtue doth a state acquire,
So all the world with scornful eyes may gaze
  On their degener'd stems, which might aspire,

As having greater power, their power to raise,
  Yet of their race the ruin do conspire,
And for their wrong-spent life with shame do end.
Kings chastised once, are not allowed t' amend.

Those who, reposing on their princely name,
  Can never give themselves to care for ought,
But for their pleasures everything would frame,
  As all were made for them, and they for nought,
Once th' earth their bodies, men will spoil their fame,
  Though, whilst they live, all for their ease be
      wrought ;
And those conceits on which they do depend
Do but betray their fortunes in the end.

This self-conceit doth so the judgment choke,
  That when with some aught well succeeds through it,
They on the same with great affection look,
  And scorn th' advice of others to admit.
Thus did brave Charles, the last Burgundian duke,
  Dear buy a battle purchased by his wit ;
By which in him such confidence was bred,
That blind presumption to confusion led.

O sacred council, quintessence of souls,
  Strength of the commonwealth, which chains the
And every danger, ere it come, controls,   [fates,
  The anchor of great realms, staff of all states !
O sure foundation which no tempest fouls,
  On which are builded the most glorious seats !
If ought with those succeed who scorn thy care,
It comes by chance, and draws them in a snare.

Thrice happy is that king, who hath the grace
  To choose a council whereon to rely,
Which loves his person, and respects his place,
  And, like to Aristides, can cast by
All private grudge, and public cares embrace,
  Whom no ambition nor base thoughts do tie—
And that they be not, to betray their seats,
The partial pensioners of foreign states.

None should but those of that grave number boast,
  Whose lives have long with many virtues shined.
As Rome respected the Patricians most,
  Use nobles first, if to true worth inclined;
Yet so, that unto others seem not lost
  All hopes to rise; for else, high hopes resigned,
Industrious virtue in her course would tire,
If not expecting honour for her hire.

But such as those a prince should most eschew,
  Who dignities do curiously affect;
A public charge those who too much pursue
  Seem to have some particular respect.
All should be godly, prudent, secret, true,
  Of whom a king his council should elect;
And he, whilst they advise of zeal and love,
Should not the number, but the best approve.

A great discretion is required to know
  What way to weigh opinions in his mind;
But ah! this doth the judgment oft o'er-throw,
  When whilst he comes within himself confined,

And of the senate would but make a show,
So to confirm that which he hath designed—
As one who only hath whereon to rest
For councillors, his thoughts, their seat his breast.

But what avails a senate in this sort,
Whose power within the capital is pent—
A blast of breath which doth for nought import,
But mocks the world with a not acted intent?
Those are the councils which great states support,
Which never are made known but by the event:
Not those where wise men matters do propose,
And fools thereafter as they please dispose.

Nor is this all which ought to be desired
In this assembly, since the kingdom's soul,
That, with a knowledge more than rare inspired,
A commonwealth, like Plato's, in a scroll
They can paint forth; but means are, too, acquired
Disorder's torrent freely to control,
And, arming with authority their lines,
To act with justice that which wit designs.

Great empress of this universal frame,
The Atlas on whose shoulders states are stayed,
Who sway'st the reins which all the world do tame,
And mak'st men good by force, with red arrayed!
Disorder's enemy, virgin without blame,
Within whose balance good and bad are weighed,
O! sovereign of all virtues, without thee
Nor peace nor war can entertained be!

Thou from confusion all things hast redeemed.
  The meeting of Amphictyons had been vain,
And all those senates which were most esteemed,
  Were 't not by thee their councils crowned remain;
And all those laws had but dead letters seemed,
  Which Solon, or Lycurgus, did ordain,
Were 't not thy sword made all alike to die,
And not the weak, while as the strong 'scaped by.

O not without great cause all th' ancients did
  Paint magistrates placed to explain the laws,
Not having hands, so bribery to forbid,
  Which them from doing right too oft withdraws;
And with a veil the judges' eyes were hid,
  Who should not see the party, but the cause.
God's deputies, which his tribunal rear,
Should have a patent, not a partial ear.

An lack of justice hath huge evils begun,
  Which by no means could be repaired again;
The famous sire of that most famous son,
  From whom, while as he sleeping did remain,
One did appeal, till that his sleep was done,
  And whom a widow did discharge to reign
Because he had not time plaints to attend,
Did lose his life for such a fault in th' end.

This justice is the virtue most divine
  Which like the King of kings shews kings inclined,
Whose sure foundations nought can undermine,
  If once within a constant breast confined:

For otherwise she cannot clearly shine,
　While as the magistrate oft changing mind
Is oft too swift, and sometimes slow to strike,
　As led by private ends, not still alike.

Use mercy freely, justice as constrained ;
　This must be done, although that be more dear,
And oft the form may make the deed disdained,
　Whilst justice tastes of tyranny too near.
One may be justly, yet in rage arraigned,
　Whilst reason ruled by passions doth appear :
Once Socrates, because o'ercome with ire,
Did from correcting one, till calmed, retire.

Those who want means their anger to assuage,
　Do oft themselves, or others, rob of breath.
Fierce Valentinian, surfeiting in rage,
　By bursting of a vein did bleed to death :
And Theodosus, still but then, thought sage,
　Caused murder thousands, whilst quite drunk with
Who, to prevent the like opprobrious crime, [wrath,
Made still suspend his edicts for a time.

Of virtuous kings all the actions do proceed
　Forth from the spring of a paternal love,
To cherish, or correct, as realms have need ;
　For which he more than for himself doth move,
Who, many a million's ease that way to breed,
　Makes sometime some his indignation prove,
And like to Codrus, would even death embrace,
If for the country's good and people's peace.

I　　　　　　　　　　　　　　　　　　　　V

This lady, that so long unarmed hath strayed,
  Now holds the balance, and doth draw the sword,
And never was more gloriously arrayed,
  Nor in short time did greater good afford;
The state which to confusion seemed betrayed,
  And could of nought but blood and wrongs record,
Lo! freed from trouble and intestine rage,
Doth boast yet to restore the golden age.

Thus doth thy father, generous prince, prepare
  A way for thee to gain immortal fame,
And lays the grounds of greatness with such care,
  That thou may'st build great works upon the same;
Then since thou art to have a field so fair,
  Whereas thou once mayst eternize thy name,
Begin, whileas a greater light thine smothers,
And learn to rule thyself ere thou rul'st others.

For still true magnanimity, we find,
  Doth harbour early in a generous breast :
To match Miltiades, whose glory shined,
  Themistocles, a child, was robbed of rest ;
Yet strive to be a monarch of thy mind,
  For as to dare great things all else detest ;
A generous emulation spurs the sp'rit,
Ambition doth abuse the courage quite.

Whilst of illustrious lives thou look'st the story,
  Abhor those tyrants which still swimmed in blood,
And follow those who, to their endless glory,
  High in their subjects' love by virtue stood ;

O! be like him who on a time was sorry
   Because that whilst he chanced to do no good
There but one day had happened to expire:
He was the world's delight, the heaven's desire.

But as by mildness some great states do gain,
   By lenity some lose that which they have.
England's sixth Henry could not live and reign,
   But, being simple, did huge foils receive:
Brave Scipio's army mutinied in Spain,
   And, by his meekness bold, their charge did leave.
O! to the state it brings great profit oft,
To be sometimes severe, and never soft.

To guide his coursers warily through the sky,
   Erst Phœbus did his phaeton require,
Since from the middle way if swerving by,
   The heavens would burn or the earth would be on
So doth 'twixt two extremes each virtue lie   [fire.
   To which the purest sp'rits ought to aspire;
He lives most sure who no extreme doth touch,
Nought would too little be, nor yet too much.

Some kings whom all men did in hatred hold,
   With avaricious thoughts whose breasts were torn,
Too basely given to feast their eyes with gold,
   Used ill and abject means, which brave minds scorn;
Such whilst they only seek, no vice controlled,
   How they may best their treasuries adorn,
Are, though like Crœsus rich, whilst wealth them
Yet still as poor as Irus in their minds.   [blinds,

And some again, as foolish fancies move,
　Who praise preposterous fondly do pursue,
Not liberal, no, but prodigal do prove,
　Then, whilst their treasures they exhausted view,
With subsidies do lose their subject's love,
　And spoil whole realms, though but t'enrich a few,
Whilst with authority their pride they cloak,
Who ought to die by smoke for selling smoke.

But O! the prince most loathed in every land
　Is one all given to lust; who hardly can
Free from some great mishap a long time stand;
　For all the world his deeds with hatred scan.
Should he who hath the honour to command
　The noblest creature, great God's image—man,
Be to the vilest vice the basest slave,
The body's plague, soul's death, and honour's grave?

That beastly monster who, retired a part,
　Amongst his concubines began to spin,
Took with the habit too a woman's heart
　And ended that which Ninus did begin.
Faint-hearted Xerxes, who did gifts impart
　To them who could devise new ways to sin,
Though backed with worlds of men, straight took
　　　the flight,
And had not courage but to see them fight.

Thus doth soft pleasure but abase the mind,
　And making one to servile thoughts descend,
Doth make the body weak, the judgment blind—
　An hateful life, an ignominious end;

Where those who did this raging tyrant bind
With virtue's chains, their triumphs to attend,
Have by that means a greater glory gained
Than all the victories which they attained.

The valorous Persian who not once but gazed
On fair Panthea's face to ease his toils,
His glory, by that continency, raised
More than by Babylon's and Lydia's spoils;
The Macedonian monarch was more praised
Than for triumphing o'er so many soils,
That of his greatest foe, though beauteous seen,
He chastely entertained the captive queen.

Thus have still-gazed-at monarchs much ado
Who, all the world's disorders to redress,
Should shine like to the sun, the which still, lo!
The more it mounts aloft, doth seem the less;
They should with confidence go freely to,
And, trusting to their worth, their will express;
Not like French Louis th' Eleventh, who did maintain
That who could not dissemble could not reign.

But still, to guard their state, the strongest bar
And surest refuge in each dangerous storm
Is to be found a gallant man of war,
With heart that dare attempt, hands to perform.
Not that they venture should their state too far,
And to each soldier's course their course conform;
The skilful pilots at the rudder sit,
Let others use their strength, and them their wit.

In Mars his mysteries to gain renown
  It gives kings glory, and assures their place;
It breeds them a respect among'st their own,
  And makes their neighbours fear to lose their grace;
Still all those should, who love to keep their crown,
  In peace prepare for war, in war for peace:
For as all fear a prince who dare attempt,
The want of courage brings one in contempt.

And, royal off-spring, who mayst high aspire,
  As one to whom thy birth high hopes assigned,
This well becomes the courage of thy sire,
  Who trains thee up according to thy kind;
He, though the world his prosperous reign admire,
  In which his subjects such a comfort find,
Hath, if the bloody art moved to embrace,
That wit then to make war, which now keeps peace.

And O! how this, dear prince, the people charms,
  Who flock about thee oft in ravished bands—
To see thee young, yet manage so thine arms,
  Have a mercurial mind and martial hands.
This exercise thy tender courage warms;
  And still true greatness but by virtue stands;
Agesilaus said no king could be
More great, unless more virtuous than he.

And though that all of thee great things expect,
  Thou, as too little, mak'st their hopes ashamed.
As he who on Olympus did detect
  The famous Theban's foot, his body framed,

By thy beginnings so we may collect
　How great thy worth by time may be proclaimed.
For who thy actions doth remark, may see
That there be many Cæsars within thee.

Though every state by long experience finds
　That greatest blessings prospering peace imparts,
As which all subjects to good order binds,
　Yet breeds this isle, still populous in all parts,
Such vigorous bodies and such restless minds,
　That they disdain to use mechanic arts,
And, being haughty, cannot live in rest,
Yea, such, when idle, are a dangerous pest.

A prudent Roman told in some few hours
　To Rome's estate what danger did redound
Then, when they razed the Carthaginian towers,
　By which, while as they stood, still means were found
With others' harms to exercise their powers ;
　The want whereof their greatness did confound,
For when no more with foreign foes embroiled,
Straight by intestine wars the state was spoiled.

No, since this soil, which with great sp'rits abounds,
　Can hardly nurse her nurslings all in peace,
Then let us keep her bosom free from wounds,
　And spend our fury in some foreign place.
There is no wall can limit now our bounds,
　But all the world will need walls in short space
To keep our troops from seizing on new thrones.
The marble chair must pass the ocean once.

What fury o'er my judgment doth prevail?
    Methinks I see all th' earth glance with our arms,
And groaning Neptune charged with many a sail;
    I hear the thundering trumpet sound th' alarms,
Whilst all the neighbouring nations do look pale,
    Such sudden fear each panting heart disarms,
To see those martial minds together gone,
The lion and the leopard in one.

I, Henry, hope with this mine eyes to feed,
    Whilst, ere thou wear'st a crown, thou wear'st a
        shield,
And when thou, making thousands once to bleed
    That dare behold thy count'nance and not yield,
Stirr'st through the bloody dust a foaming steed.
    An interested witness in the field,
I may amongst those bands thy grace attend,
And be thy Homer when the wars do end.

But stay, where fliest thou, Muse, so far astray?
    And whilst affection doth thy course command,
Dar'st thus above thy reach attempt a way
    To court the heir of Albion's warlike land,
Who gotten hath, his generous thoughts to sway,
    A royal gift out of a royal hand,
And hath before his eyes that type of worth,
That star of state, that pole which guides the north.

Yet o'er thy father, lo, such is thy fate,
    Thou hast this vantage which may profit thee—
An orphaned infant, settled in his seat,
    He greater than himself could never see,

Where thou may'st learn by him the art of state,
  And by another what thyself should'st be,
Whilst that which he had only but heard told,
In all his course thou practised may'st behold,

And this advantage long may'st thou retain,
  By which to make thee blest the heavens conspire,
And labour of his worth to make thy gain,
  To whose perfections thou may'st once aspire ;
When as thou shew'st thyself, whilst thou dost reign,
  A son held worthy of so great a sire,
And with his sceptres and the people's hearts,
Dost still inherit his heroic parts.

OLYMPIAS
BEFORE EXECUTION.*

Can I be she whom all the world admired
As the most happy queen that reigned below,
Whom all the planets have to plague conspired,
Of fickle fortune's course the power to shew?
No, no, not I, for what could me control
Or force me thus t' attend another's will,
Since I despise the prison of my soul
Where it disdains t' abide in bondage still?
Ah! whilst vain pomp transported fancies fed,
The jealous gods my state to grudge did tempt—

---

* Upon the death by poison of Alexander the Great at
Babylon, his captains divided the conquered provinces among
themselves, and decided to rule as regents, awaiting the birth of
Alexander's expected heir. Presently, however, moved by
personal ambition, these captains plotted against and overthrew
each other. In this struggle Olympias, the mother of Alexander,
took an active part, endeavouring to hold Macedonia itself for
her son's child by his queen Roxana. In the course of her
campaign she put to death her husband Philip's natural son
Arideus and his queen Eurydice, who had pretended to the
crown. Having, however, by this and some other cruelties,
lost the favour of the people, she was, a little later, captured by
Cassander, one of the rival captains and her son's poisoner, and
was put to death. Cassander next caused Roxana and her son to
be murdered, and also, soon afterwards, Hercules, Alexander's
natural son. By this series of crimes he set himself at last on
his master's throne. *The Alexandraean Tragedy* is framed upon
these incidents.

My state which envy once, and reverence, bred,
Though now it breed but pity and contempt.
Olympias once high as Olympus stood,
The wife of Philip, Alexander's mother,
Who matched Alcides' and Achilles' blood
To breed a man more worth than both together.
Am I the woman whose majestic state
Seemed once so happy to deceived conceits?
I, I am she, and never yet more great
Than at this present, even in spite of fates.
A double bondage long did burden me,
I to myself, myself to fortune thrall;
But now captivity hath set me free,
Who could not rise till first I had a fall.
A sp'rit, whilst it prosperity benumbs,
Scarce like the self can to the world appear,
But then, when virtue every cross o'ercomes,
True greatness shines most bright in glory's sphere.
Our treasure, now I see, consists no more
Without ourselves, in th' eye-betraying shows,
But in the breast's inestimable store,
Which neither time entombs nor power o'erthrows.
O never were my thoughts enlarged till now
To mark myself, and quintessence my mind;
For, long, a prey to pride, I know not how,
A mist of fancies made my judgment blind.
As those who dream sweet dreams, whilst wak'st at last,
Do find their error when their eyes find light,
Free from the slumb'ring of my fortune past,
I now arise to judge of all things right.
That cloud of pomp whose smoke me shadowed once,

Lo, now removed, unmasks my life too late,
And now I see that sceptres, crowns, and thrones
Are burdenous badges of a dangerous state.
O happy woman, of true pleasure sure,
Who in the country leads a guiltless life,
From fortune's reach retired, obscure, secure,
Though not a queen, yet a contented wife!
Thy mate, more dear to thee than is the light,
Though low in state, loves in a high degree,
And with his presence still to bless thy sight,
Doth scorn great courts whilst he lives courting thee.
And as thou wound'st him not with hid disgrace,
He with no jealous thought doth rack thy breast:
Thus both lie down to rest, and rise in peace;
Then, if they strive, they strive who should love best.
What though thou have not, as the mighty ones,
Thy neck surcharged with chains — Ah, chains
    indeed !—
Nor ears weighed down with oriental stones,
Nor robes whose worth may admiration breed;
So want'st thou that which we have ever had,
Sad miscontentments, jealousy, and spite,
And though thy back be not with purple clad
Thy thoughts are decked with innocencies white.
As birds whose cage of gold the sight deceives,
Do seem to sing whilst they do wail their state,
So, with the mighty matched, made glorious slaves,
We happy seem, whilst we but curse our fate.
That bliss whose show in us vain eyes doth please,
Makes thee indeed with pleasure spend thy breath,
Who liv'st, while young, in mirth, while aged, in ease,

And know'st not what it is to die till death.
Ah ! since I lived I always did but die,
When seeming happy, then most wretched still.
Whilst dazzling with vain pomp each vulgar eye,
What strange mishaps did me with anguish fill !
The fates with fortune from my birth conspired
To make my life a pattern of their might ;
For both my parents from the world retired
When I had scarcely looked upon the light.
The world may judge how I was justly grieved
Whilst angry Philip sought for my disgrace—
A thing which once I scarce could have believed—
And unto Cleopatra gave my place.
Then though I long, as desperate of relief,
For his offence afflicted had my mind,
Yet did his sudden death augment my grief –
He was my husband, though he was unkind.
And when my son's rare deeds, which fame doth
    sound,
The world with wonder, ravished me with joy,
Those, as himself, who would all his confound,
To compass me did spite and power employ.
Yet stood my courage when my fortune fell,
And still I toiled to persecute his foes,
That some might fall down who too much did swell,
Their blood in marble regist'ring my woes.
That which I purposed, long so prospered too,
That some of them did try, by torments strange,
All what a woman's just disdain could do
Whilst spurred by jealousy, spite, and revenge.
But this arch-traitor, ruler of the rest,

Who thirsts to drink the blood of all our race,
Even then, with us when all succeeded best,
Did compass me with ruin and disgrace.
Such was the tenor of my fortune past,
Whose least mishap had made another burst;
First orphaned, widowed, and unchilded last,
A daughter, wife, and mother all accurst.
Heavens plague Cassander! Let that base wretch try
That Jove his judgment but a while defers;
And let his wife bewail as well as I—
I murdered for my son, and she by hers.
Even as th' incestuous Theban's monstrous brood,
So may thy sons contend with mutual wounds,
And never let thy house be free from blood
Till banished quite from this usurpèd bounds.
Thus, notwithstanding of my wonted power,
To me, save wishes, nothing doth remain;
But though condemned to die, yet, at this hour,
Should I begin to curse and to complain?
No, no, that custom best becomes poor souls
Whose resolution cannot climb more high;
But I, whose courage that base course controls,
Must triumph still, whatever state I try.
Death is the port where all may refuge find,
The end of labour, entry unto rest.
Death hath the bounds of misery confined,
Whose sanctuary shrouds affliction best.
To suffer, oft, with a courageous heart,
It doth deserve more praise than deeds most known:
For in our actions fortune hath some part,
But in our sufferings all things are our own.

Lo, now I loath the world and worldly things,
Of which I both have proved the best and worst.
The apprehended death great comfort brings,
And hath no cross but that it should be forced.
O hear me now, dear son, if that thy ghost
May leave th' Elysian fields to look on me—
Of all things else this doth content me most,
That from this time I may remain with thee.
And blush not now to see thy mother's end;
My death in glory with thy life shall strive;
It, as a captive, fortune shall attend,
That, as thy fellow, followed thee alive.

BRUTUS AND PORTIA.

THE TRAGEDY OF JULIUS CÆSAR—ACT III., SCENE 2.

Brut. My dearest half, my comfort, my delight,
Of whom one smile may sweeten all my sours,
Thou in my bosom used to pour thy sp'rit,
And where I was didst spare affliction's powers.
When broils domestic did disturb thy rest,
Then still, till finding, feigning some relief,
Thou with calm words disguised a stormy breast,
Joys frankly sharing, and engrossing grief.
Still tend'ring me with a respective care,
What might offend was by no means made known,
But—with love's colours all things painted fair—
What might have made me glad was gladly shown.
How com'st thou then thy courage thus to lose,
That thou canst look so sad, and in my sight?
Lend me, dear love, a portion of thy woes!
A burden when divided doth grow light.
I see the roses fading in thy face,
The lilies languish, violets take their place.

Por. Thou hast, dear lord, prevented my design,
Which was to ask of thee what makes me pale.
If Phœbus had no light could Phœbe shine?
No, with the cause of force th' effects must fail.
The mirror but gives back as it receives
By just resemblance the objected form,
And what impression the engraver leaves

The wax retains, still to the stamp conform.
I am the mirror which reflects thy mind,
As forced from thoughts, or flowing from thine eyes;
I take the state in which thy state I find;
Such is my colour as thy count'nance dyes.
Then how can I rejoice whilst thou art sad,
Whose breast of all thy crosses is the scroll?
I am still as thou art, if grieved or glad,
Thy body's shadow, th' essence of thy soul.
On that great planet which divides the years
Of fields inferior as the fruit depend,
And as it vanish doth, or pleased appears,
In th' earth's cold bosom life begins or ends;
Sun of my soul, so I subsist by thee,
Whose shining virtue leads me as a thrall;
From care-bred clouds if that thy face be free
I rise in joys, but if thou faint I fall.
 Brut. With all my course this count'nance best
  accords,
Who, as you know, yet never from my birth
Light gestures used, nor did delight in words
Whose pleasant strains were only tuned to mirth.
My melancholy nature feeds on cares,
Whilst smothered sorrow by a habit smokes.
A thoughtful breast, when burdened with affairs,
Doth make a silent mouth and speaking looks.
As for my paleness, it imports but good;
The body's humbling doth exalt the mind,
When fatness, come from food, but serves for food:
In fattest bodies leanest sp'rits we find.
Ah! since I saw the abhorred Thessalia's bounds
K   V

All drenched with blood of senators and kings,
As if my soul yet smarted in their wounds,
A secret sorrow oftentimes me stings.
But since thy father, braving pain with blows,
In the most hideous form affronted death,
To him my mind a sad remembrance owes,
Which sorrow shall exact whilst I have breath.
Yet grieve I that I gave thee cause of grief,
Who thoughtst some new mishap did me dismay;
To such old sores one worst can give relief,
But time in end may wear my woes away.

   Por. Why shouldst thou so from me thy thoughts
     conceal?—
From thine own soul between whose breasts thou
     sleep'st,
To whom, though shown, thou dost them not reveal,
But in thyself more inwardly them keep'st?
And thou canst hardly hide thyself from me,
Who soon in thee each alteration spy.
I can comment on all that comes from thee;
True love still looks with a suspicious eye.
Within our bosom rests not every thought
Tuned by a sympathy of mutual love?
Thou marr'st the music if thou change in ought,
Which, when distempered, I do quickly prove.
Soul of my soul, unfold what is amiss!
Some great disaster all my thoughts divine,
Whose curiousness may be excused in this,
Since it concerns thy state and therefore mine.

   Brut. I wonder that thou dost thy frailty show!
By nature women have been curious still.

And yet till now thou never craved to know
More than I pleased to speak of my free will.
Nought save the wife a man within the walls,
Nor ought save him without she should embrace,
And it not comely is, but th' one enthralls,
When any sex usurps another's place.
Dear, to their wonted course thy cares inure :
I may have matters which import the state,
Whose opening up might my disgrace procure,
Whose weight for female thoughts would be too great.

   Por. I was not, Brutus, matched with thee to be
A partner only of thy board and bed :
Each servile w—— in these might equal me,
Who but for pleasure or for wealth did wed.
No, Portia spoused thee minding to remain
Thy fortune's partner, whether good or ill.
By love's strict bonds, whilst mutual duties chain,
Two breasts must hold one heart, two souls one will.
Those whom just Hymen voluntar'ly binds
Betwixt them should communicate all things,
But chiefly that which most doth move the minds,
Whence either pleasure or displeasure springs.
If thus thou seek thy sorrows to conceal
Through a disdain or a mistrust of me,
Then to the world what way can I reveal
How great a matter I would do for thee ?
And though our sex too talkative be deemed,
As those whose tongues import our greatest powers,
For secrets still bad treasurers esteemed,
Of others greedy, prodigal of ours ;
Good education may reform defects,

And this may lead me to a virtuous life—
Whilst such rare patterns generous worth respects;
I Cato's daughter am, and Brutus' wife.
Yet would I not repose my trust in ought,
Still thinking that thy cross was great to bear,
Till I my courage to a trial brought,
Which suffering for thy cause can nothing fear.
For first to try how that I could comport
With stern affliction's sp'rit-enfeebling blows,
Ere I would seek to vex thee in this sort,
To whom my soul a duteous reverence owes,
Lo, here a wound which makes me not to smart:
No, I rejoice that thus my strength is known;
Since thy distress strikes keeper in my heart
Thy grief, life's joy, makes me neglect mine own.
 Brut. Thou must, dear love, that which thou
  sought'st receive.
Thy heart so high a sail in storms still bears
That thy great courage doth reserve to have
Our enterprise entrusted to thine ears.
This magnanimity prevails so far
That it my resolution must control,
And of my bosom doth the depths unbar
To lodge thee in the centre of my soul.
Thou seest in what estate the state now stands,
Of whose strong pillars Cæsar spoiled the best,
Whilst, by his own, preventing others' hands,
Our famous father fell amongst the rest.
That proud usurper fondly doth presume
To re-erect detested Tarquin's throne,
Thus the world's mistress, all-commanding Rome,

Must entertain no minion now but one.
All those brave minds who mark where he doth tend,
Swell with disdain their country's scorn to see ;
And I am one of those who soon intend,
His death or mine procured, to be made free.

    Por. And without me canst thou resolve so soon
To try the danger of a doubtful strife ?
As if despaired, and always but undone,
Of me grown weary ; weary of thy life !
Yet since thou thus thy rash design hast shown,
Leave Portia's portion, venture not her part,
Endanger nought but that which is thine own :—
Go where thou lik'st, I will hold still thy heart.
But lest by holding of thy best part back
The other, perished, aggravate my groans—
Who would be so thought guilty of thy wrack ?—
Take all thy treasure to the seas at once.
Like Asia's monarch's wife, who with short hairs,
Sad signs of bondage, passed still where he passed,
To wear away or bear away thy cares
I'll follow thee and of thy fortune taste.   [brued,
These hands, which were with mine own blood im-
To strike another may more strength afford.
At least, when thou by th' enemies art pursued,
I'll set myself betwixt thee and each sword.
But if too great a privilege I claim,
Whose actions all should be disposed by thee,
Ah ! pardon, Brutus, and but only blame
This stream of passions that transported me.

    Brut. Thou ask'st what thou shouldst give.
    Forgive, dear mate,

This venturous course of mine, which must have place
Though it make fortune tyrant of our state,
Whose fickle footsteps virtue grieves to trace.
And wonder not though thus to thee I prove,
Since private duties now all power have lost;
I weigh not glory, profit, pleasure, love,
Nor what respect may now import me most.
So to the land of which I hold my life
I may perform that work which I intend,
Let me be called unkind unto my wife;
Yea, worst of all, ingrate unto my friend.
As an instinct by nature makes us know,
There are degrees of duty to be passed,
Of which the first unto the gods we owe,
The next t' our country, to our friends the last.
From Rome of old proud tyrants bent to drive,
Did th' author of my race, with ardent zeal,
Make those to die whom he had made to live,
And spoiled himself to raise the commonweal.
To settle that which Cæsar now o'erthrows,
Though, virtue's nursery, stately whilst it stood,
He, with the tyrant interchanging blows,
On glory's altar offered fame his blood.
And did that man, to cross the common foe,
Then damn his sons to death, and with dry eyes?
And is his special heir degenered so
In abject bondage that he basely lies?
No, his posterity his name not stains,
But even to tread his steps doth fast draw near:
Yet of his sp'rit in us some spark remains,
Who more than life our liberty hold dear.

Por. Then prosecute thy course, for I protest,
Though with some grief, my soul the same approves.
This resolution doth become thy breast
In honour's sphere, where heavenly virtue moves.
And do this enterprise no more defer;
What thee contents, to me contentment brings.
I to my life thy safety do prefer,
But hold thy honour dear above all things.
It would but let the world my weakness see
If I sought my delights, not thy desires.
Though grief it give, and threaten death to me,
Go, follow forth that which thy fame requires.
Though nature, sex, and education breed
No power in me with such a purpose even,
I must lend help to this intended deed
If vows and prayers may penetrate the heaven.
But difficulties huge my fancy finds:
Nought save the success can defray my fear.
Ah! fortune always frowns on worthy minds,
As hating all who trust in ought save her.
Yet I despair not but thou may'st prevail,
And by this course, to ease my present groans,
I this advantage have which cannot fail—
I'll be a freeman's wife, or else be none's.
For, if all prosper not as we pretend,
And that the heavens Rome's bondage do decree,
Straight with thy liberty my life shall end,
Who have no comfort but what comes from thee.
My father hath me taught what way to die,
By which, if hindered from encount'ring death,
Some other means I, though more strange, must try;

For, after Brutus, none shall see me breathe.

Brut. Thou for my cause all others erst did'st leave,
But now forsak'st thyself to join with me.
O'er generous love no power weak passions have ;
Against thy mind thou dost with mine agree.
I'll, since by thee approved, securely go
And vilipend the dangers of this life.
Heavens make my enterprise to prosper so
That I may once prove worthy such a wife!
But ah ! of all thy words those grieve me most
Which brag me with the dating of thy days !
What though I in so good a cause were lost?
None flies the fate which stablished for him stays.
Do not defraud the world of thy rare worth,
But of thy Brutus the remembrance love ;
From this fair prison strive not to break forth
Till first the fates have forced thee to remove.

Por. The heavens I fear have our confusion sworn,
Since this ill age can with no good accord.
Thou and my father, ah ! should have been born
When virtue was advanced and vice abhorred.
Then, ere the light of virtue was declined,
Your worth had reverenced been, not thrown away,
Where now ye both have but in darkness shined
As stars of night, that had been suns by day.

Brut. My treasure, strive to pacify thy breast,
Lest sorrows but sinistrously presage
That which thou would'st not wish. And hope the best,
Though virtue now must act on fortune's stage.

WILLIAM DRUMMOND.

WILLIAM DRUMMOND.

With one exception the Scottish poets of mark of the Jacobean period were something more than simply men of letters. Courtiers, statesmen, or, as in the case of the later Montrose, soldiers, the main interests of their lives lay in the world of action, and poetry was with them either the solace of hours of retirement or the outcome of experience gained in active life. William Drummond, alone of them all, can be said to have lived a life devoted to the art of poetry. To this circumstance may possibly, to some extent, be attributed the fact that of all the Scottish poets of that time he, without question, holds the highest place.

Hawthornden estate lies on the banks of the North Esk, near Lasswade, about seven miles from Edinburgh. The mansion-house, a picturesque mass of ancient roofs and gables, rises among its trees high on the cliff edge overhanging the stream. The more modern part of the house was built by the poet himself, but the rest, ivy-mantled now, and ruinous, is believed to be at least six hundred years old. Under its foundations, hewn in the solid rock of the cliff-face,

arc caves said to have been places of refuge of Scottish
patriots during the wars of Bruce and David II. Not
far distant, on the other side of the rocky glen, stands
Roslin Castle, the ruined stronghold of the St. Clairs,
and Roslin Chapel, perhaps the richest gem of ancient
ecclesiastical architecture in the country, with, on the
moor above them, the scene where in one day, about
the year 1299, three English armies were defeated in
succession by Sir John Comyn and Sir Simon Fraser.
These surroundings, with the romantic chasm of the
Esk itself, and the river brawling down its bed far
below, make Hawthornden to the present hour exactly
such a spot as might stir the imaginings of a poet.

Here on December 13, 1585, William Drummond
was born. His father, John Drummond, the first
Drummond of Hawthornden, was second son of Sir
Robert Drummond of Carnock in Stirlingshire, head
of a branch of the Drummonds, barons of Stobhall in
Perthshire, one of whose daughters was mother of
James I. The poet's mother was Susannah Fowler,
sister of William Fowler, a person of some literary
attainment, who afterwards became private secretary
to the queen. John Drummond probably met her at
the Scottish court, where he himself presently became
gentleman-usher to the king, and obtained the honour
of knighthood. Eldest of a family of seven, William
Drummond was educated at the High School and at
the University of Edinburgh, taking his degree in
1605. As he did not intend to push his fortunes
at court, like the many young Scotsmen who followed
James VI. to England, and as he did not mean to

enter the church, the only profession for which
Edinburgh University could then qualify, he was
sent to Paris and Bourges to study law. By the
death of his father, however, in 1610, he became
master of independent means, and forthwith, giving
up all thought of pursuing a career for which he had
little liking, he retired to Hawthornden. That
romantic spot was thenceforth his home ; to its situation and surroundings he probably owed much of
what he presently became ; and by his residence there
he made it—what is now its chief claim to regard—a
shrine of poetic and literary memories.

After this retirement to Hawthornden the poet's
life appears to have been for most part that of the
quiet country gentleman. His library in 1610 contained 267 Latin books, 35 Greek, 11 Hebrew, 61
Italian, 8 Spanish, 120 French, and 50 English. A
large part of these he appears to have himself read in
the original, and he added judiciously to their number,
till in 1627 he was able to make a gift to the library
of his beloved Alma Mater of 500 choice volumes—
a collection which still remains one of the most valued
treasures of Edinburgh University.

From the sequestered retreat at Hawthornden
Drummond first attracted literary notice after the
death of Prince Henry. Upon that sad event, which
occurred in 1612, he, like many others of his time,
composed an elegy—*Teares for the Death of Mœliades.*
This was the name which the young heir of the crown
had been accustomed to assume in his sports and
masquerades. The elegy, published by Andro Hart

at Edinburgh, went through three editions within a
year, and led to Drummond's life-long friendship with
Sir William Alexander, then at the height of his
reputation.

Notwithstanding the success of this little piece,
nothing further from Drummond's pen appeared till
1616. In the intervening period had happened what
from its consequences must be considered the great
event of the poet's life. He had fallen in love, and had
wooed, won, and sadly lost the object of his affections.
The lady was a daughter of Cunningham of Barns, in
Fife. Her Christian name has not come down to us,
and nearly all that is known of the affair is given in
four lines by Bishop Sage, the writer of the biography
prefixed to the edition of Drummond's works of 1711.
The poet, it appears, was successful in his suit,
receiving a warm return of his affections, "but when
the day for the marriage was appointed, and all things
ready for the solemnization of it, the young lady took
a fever, and was suddenly snatched away by it, to his
great grief and sorrow."

This experience, with the wakening of feeling and the
tearing of heart-strings which it involved, did more
than anything else in his life to stir and exalt the
genius of the poet. Its effect was both deep and
lasting, and its immediate result was most valuable
to literature. In the flush of his hopes as a lover
he had written a number of poems—songs, sonnets,
and madrigals—descriptive of his passion; and under
the cloud of his despair he shut himself up at
Hawthornden, and, brooding on his grief, pro-

duced another series recording his later emotions. The whole collection he published in 1616, the year of Shakespeare's death, under the title of *Poems, Amorous, Funerall, Divine, Pastorall.* Between the lines of this volume the reader can decipher the story of the poet's love and loss.

In May of the following year King James paid his first visit to Scotland since ascending the English throne. Universal rejoicing and much panegyric, written and spoken, marked the occasion. But apart from its political issues the event is now chiefly remembered by the poem written on it by Drummond. This production, *Forth Feasting, A Panegyric to the King's Most Excellent Majesty*, apparently brought no mark of approbation, and no reward, from James himself; but it definitely fixed attention on the new poet, whose reputation had been gradually growing in London. First the veteran Michael Drayton opened correspondence with him in most cordial terms; then —the event in Drummond's life which has appealed most to popular fancy—Ben Jonson, the autocrat of literary London at that time, on his great walking tour to the country of his own ancestors, paid a visit to the poet's home.

This visit probably occurred about Christmas in 1618, and tradition runs that Drummond, expecting his guest, was sitting under the ancient sycamore which still stands in front of the house, when down the avenue from the high road trudged the burly figure of Jonson. Drummond, it is said, stepped forward with the words "Welcome, welcome, royal

Ben !" To which Jonson replied, "Thank ye, thank ye, Hawthornden." Whereupon the two laughed, turned into the house, and sealed their friendship with the good cheer there waiting.

While Jonson stayed with him, Drummond kept a note of some of the great man's sayings, chiefly gossip and criticism regarding his contemporaries. A fragment of this MS., printed in the 1711 edition of Drummond's works, has furnished foundation for an attack by Gifford, Jonson's biographer, upon his hero's Scottish host, Drummond being accused of malignity, playing the spy, and the like. The entire MS., however, has been more recently discovered, and was published in the *Transactions of the Society of Scottish Antiquaries* (iv. 241); and the summing up of the whole question, now possible, appears to be that, while Drummond was perhaps unwise in letting it remain on record that the burly and somewhat rough and gross personality of Jonson grated upon his own more delicate and refined nature, he has said nothing in his few lines of summary regarding his guest which was not evidently true, while, as for the record of Ben Jonson's own remarks on contemporaries, we can only wish we had more of it.*

For several years after this visit Drummond lived an uneventful life at Hawthornden, his melancholy for the loss of his mistress, as well as a serious illness which carried him to the gates of death, turning his

---

* It was reserved for a later Johnson to be chronicled on his Scottish tour with the painstaking minuteness of a Boswell.

muse more and more into a religious vein. Of these
years the poetic fruits appeared in 1623. That was a
year of gloom and fear in Scotland. Famine lay on
the country, and a large part of the population was
cut down. Strange lights too—blazing stars, fire-
flaughts, and flaming dragons—seen in the heavens
seemed to forebode disaster. God, in the opinion of
many, was about to punish the wickedness of men—
to visit with His wrath such enormities, for instance,
as the king's recent introduction of Episcopacy to
Scotland, and the proposed Spanish marriage of
Prince Charles. In these circumstances the appearance of Drummond's *Flowers of Sion*, together with
his grave and beautiful prose essay, *The Cypress
Grove*, both dealing chiefly with death and the vanity
of human life, must have touched a sympathetic chord
in the national temper of the time.

With this publication Drummond's poetical career
may be said to have closed. He did not cease to
write verse, but what he wrote was slight of purpose,
and all that was published during his life, excepting,
indeed, an *Entertainment*, or set of speeches, written
for King Charles's coronation visit to Edinburgh in
1633, was a commendatory sonnet, or occasional set
of lines written once in a while to introduce the
publications of friends.

Of the last twenty-six years of the poet's life it is
only necessary here to sum the facts. After 1623 his
chief connection with poetry appears to have been in
correspondence with friends like Sir Robert Ker and
Michael Drayton. A visit which he is supposed to
L.   V

have paid to the continent was probably cut short by
the war with France in 1626 ; and in all likelihood it
was this experience, aided perhaps by a suggestion
from the fertile brain of his friend Sir William
Alexander, which turned his mind to the prospecting
of various engines of war.   For a variety of these,
at anyrate — carbines, bayonets, ship's logs, telescopes,
and a perpetual-motion machine — he obtained a
patent that autumn.   In 1627 he made his gift to
the library of Edinburgh University ; and in 1632 he
married.   The lady, Elizabeth Logan, was, according
to one tradition, daughter of the parish minister of
Eddlestone, about ten miles south of Hawthornden,
but in the family papers she is stated to have been
sister to James Logan of Mountlothian, and grand-
daughter to Sir Robert Logan of Restalrig, famous
through his connection with the Gowrie conspiracy.
Drummond was attracted to her, it is said, by her
close resemblance to his early mistress.   He became
by her the father of five sons and four daughters.

About the same time occurred the scandal regarding the suppressed earldom of Stratherne.   It was a
long story, involving questions of the legitimacy of
the children of Robert II., and seeming in these
troublous times to threaten some danger to the
throne.   Regarding the difficulty, Drummond, by
way of warning, addressed to Charles a paper entitled
Considerations to the King.   Possibly this production
was, like the patent for military engines, owed to
the suggestion of Drummond's friend, Lord Stirling,
but pamphlet and patent together mark the be-

ginning of the poet's interest in the political affairs
of his time. In the following year, when Charles
came northward for his coronation, Drummond wrote
his *Entertainment* for the royal reception in Edinburgh. Neither his addresses to royalty, however,
nor his merit as a poet ever brought him any recog-
nition at the hands of the king.

Near the same period, stimulated by a correspondence with the Earl of Perth, representative of
the ancient house of Stobhall, and therefore head
of the name of Drummond, the poet began his
*History of the Lives and Reigns of the Five Jameses,
Kings of Scotland,* a work which was finished about
1644, and was published in 1655, after its author's
death.

But with the coronation visit of Charles to Scotland
the real troubles of the country had begun, and from
that time forth Drummond became more and more
engrossed in political events. To protect himself and
his property he signed the National Covenant of
1638; but his sympathies were upon the side of the
court, and, in the royalist interest, among various
squibs and epigrams, he wrote and circulated several
tracts. The chief of these were *Irene (Peace), or a
Remonstrance for Concord, Amity, and Love amongst
His Majesty's Subjects,* and Σκιαμαχία *(Shadow-fighting),
or a Defence of a Petition tendered to the Lords of the
Council of Scotland by certain Noblemen and Gentlemen.* The former of these was an endeavour to
advocate moderation on both sides at the first signing
of the Covenant against the king; the second, of

later date, in 1643, was chiefly a denunciation of the irksome domination of the Presbyterian clergy in all affairs, public and private, of Scotland at that time.

The great civil war was by this time raging between the king and the parliament in England. Marston Moor was fought in July, 1644, and Charles received his final defeat at Naseby in June, 1645. Between these dates the Marquis of Montrose effected his brilliant series of victories in Scotland. After the crowning triumph of the royalist general at Kilsyth, Drummond, who was a personal friend, hastened to send him congratulations, and, in return, received his protection; and one of the last acts of Montrose before leaving the country at the final command of Charles was the courtly and gracious one of sending the old poet a letter of kindly thanks and farewell.

Later, in 1648, when King Charles lay a prisoner at Carisbrooke in the Isle of Wight, and a new attempt to rescue him, made by the "Engagers," was rekindling the flames of war, Drummond again took up his pen to help the movement. Strangely enough, however, notwithstanding this and his former repeated appeals in the cause of royalty, he appears to have been in no way molested by the democratic government in power, and was left throughout in quiet possession of his house and estate.

To him and to the other royalists of the country the climax of horror came in January, 1649, when Charles laid his head on the block at Whitehall. Throughout his life Drummond had been an ardent Royalist: constantly, alike in the time of the learned

James and of the luckless Charles, he had in poetry
and in prose supported the courtly side; and now,
at what seemed the end of all he thought noble in
the state, he probably did not much care to survive.
There appears no reason, save the statement of his
biographer of 1711, to believe that the shock of the
news actually hastened Drummond's death; but the
fact remains that the poet survived the king only
some ten months. "He died," says Bishop Sage,
"the 4th of December, wanting only nine days of
64 years of age, to the great grief and loss of all
learned and good men; and was honourably buried
in his own aisle in the church of Lasswade, near to
his house of Hawthornden." There, amid the ruins,
under its own stone arch, the poet's grave is still to
be seen. His family at his death consisted of two
sons and a daughter, to the descendants of whom
Hawthornden still belongs.

At the instance of the poet's brother-in-law, Sir John
Scot of Scot's Tarvet, the first collected edition of
Drummond's prose works was published at London
in 1755. The poetry was published in the following
year, the editor being Edward Phillips, nephew of
John Milton : and it has been supposed that the
author of "Lycidas" and "Il Penseroso" inspired
the preface. This describes Drummond's genius as
"the most polite and verdant that ever the Scottish
nation produced," and sets Drummond on a level
with "Tasso and the choicest of the English poets."
Next, in 1684, there was printed at Edinburgh a
curious Dog-Latin farcical poem of the cast of

humour of "Christ's Kirk on the Green," entitled
Polemo-Medinia inter Vitervam et Nebernam (*i.e.,*
"The Midden-Fecht between Scotstarvet and New-
barns"). This, when reprinted at Oxford by the
future Bishop Gibson in 1691, was definitely stated
to be by Drummond. Of late the authorship has
been disputed, chiefly on the ground that no mention
of the piece occurred during Drummond's lifetime,
and that no allusion to it appears in the poet's MSS.
But the evidence seems to favour its authenticity,
which was never denied by the poet's family ; and
for several decades this was the most popular of all
Drummond's productions. An enlarged edition of
the poet's works—prose and verse—with a life prefixed, was issued under the hands of Bishop Sage
and Thomas Ruddiman in 1711. No later edition
of the prose has been printed, but the standard
edition of the poetry is that edited for the Maitland
Club by Lord Dundrennan and David Irving in
1832. Later editions are those of Peter Cunningham
in 1833, and of W. B. Turnbull in 1856. Of the
poet's life, the fullest and best account is that by
Professor Masson, published by Messrs. Macmillan
& Co., London, in 1873.

Of Drummond's prose work little need here be said.
His history lacks value from the fact that it represents no original research, but is merely a *réchauffé*
of previously known facts, tinged by the personal
politics of the writer. Nor is there evidence that his
minor tracts exercised any influence on the political
movements with which they dealt. Regarding the

Cypress Grove, however, a different criticism has to be recorded. An essay on the folly of the fear of death, it has been termed by a competent critic one of the noblest prose poems in literature. Full of a mournful music, and written in a pure and lofty strain, language and thought in its pages together roll on, bearing the soul away irresistibly from the littlenesses and petty troubles of life to the consideration of a philosophy regarding death which is as consolatory and ennobling as it is grave and beautiful. For its high qualities, says the poet's biographer, "it surpasses any similar piece of old English prose known to me, unless it be here and there, perhaps a passage in some of the English divines at their best, or Sir Thomas Browne of Norwich in the finest parts of his *Urn-Burial.*" It remains, indeed, both in conception and execution, probably the greatest thing which Drummond did.

Drummond's poetry, though it is limited in range, was certainly the finest English poetry of its time. Shakespeare, it is believed, laid down his pen in 1613, and Milton took up his in 1625. Between these dates Drummond produced in succession his "Tears on the Death of Moeliades," his "Poems, Amorous, Funeral, and Divine," his "Forth Feasting," and his "Flowers of Sion"—all of his poetical work, excepting a stray sonnet or two, which was published during his lifetime. To this work there was no rival, unless we turn to dramatic composition, in which the master of the period was Drummond's famous visitor, Ben Jonson. The chief characteristics of

Drummond's verse are its lustrous beauty and its
melodious sweetness. For these qualities it has been
termed Spenserian, but Spenser was not its model.
Just then the Italian poets were anew attracting
attention in this country. In Scotland a new translation of Petrarch had recently been made by
Drummond's uncle, Secretary Fowler, and Ariosto
had been similarly treated by Stewart of Baldynneis.
Drummond, moreover, was familiar with the Italian
poets in the original, and it was he who reintroduced
into England the fine Italian vein in which he was
presently copied and surpassed by Milton. His
"Tears for the Death of Mœliades" is said to have
afforded the model for Milton's "Lycidas"; and it
has been suggested further * that "if we had had no
Drummond we should never have seen the delicacies
of Comus, L'Allegro, and Il Penseroso." Drummond
has been called the Scottish Petrarch, and his
sonnets are still held to rank immediately after those
of Shakespeare, Milton, and Wordsworth. If he
appears to lack vigour and originality, as has sometimes been said, that lack is more than atoned for
by the wonderful sensuous richness and perfection
of his work. His genius, it is true, seems to have
been unfitted for the production of any long-sustained
composition, but so also, later, was the genius of
Robert Burns, and it may well be doubted whether
the yard-measure serves as any very valuable criterion
of poetic merits.

Altogether, as might perhaps have been expected,

* Pinkerton's *Ancient Scottish Poems.*

Drummond's work presents a reflection of his life—
a life without struggle or vehemence, inspired with
a lofty idealism, and tinged in its finer part with a
gentle melancholy. In his verse is to be seen the
dawn of the philosophy and feeling of modern poetry
—a light which was to be obscured for a time by
the troubles of the second Reformation. By the poet
of Hawthornden the taste for nature and the power
of rich natural description which have always been
characteristic of the best Scottish poets were united
to an ease and grace in the use of the English
tongue for which he had no rival among either his
predecessors or contemporaries. To leave detail,
Drummond indeed must be admitted not only to
have been the greatest Scottish poet of his own age,
but to be entitled to rank among the great English
poets of all time.

POEMS:

AMOROUS, FUNERAL, DIVINE.

FIRST PART

SONNET.

IN my first years, and prime yet not at height,
    When sweet conceits my wits did entertain,
    Ere beauty's force I knew, or false delight,
Or to what oar she did her captives chain,
Led by a sacred troop of Phœbus' train,
I first began to read, then loved to write,
And so to praise a perfect red and white,
But, God wot, wist not what was in my brain.
Love smiled to see in what an awful guise
I turned those antiques of the age of gold,
And, that I might more mysteries behold,
He set so fair a volume to mine eyes,
    That I (quires closed which dead, dead sighs but
        breath)
    Joy on this living book to read my death.

SONNET.

I KNOW that all beneath the moon decays,
And what by mortals in this world is brought
In Time's great periods shall return to nought;
That fairest states have fatal nights and days;
I know how all the Muse's heavenly lays,
With toil of sp'rit which are so dearly bought,
As idle sounds, of few or none are sought,
And that nought lighter is than airy praise.
I know frail beauty 's like the purple flower
To which one morn oft birth and death affords;
That love a jarring is of minds' accords,
Where sense and will invassal reason's power.
   Know what I list, this all can not me move,
   But that, O me! I both must write and love.

SONNET.

THAT learned Grecian, who did so excel
In knowledge passing sense, that he is named
Of all the after-worlds divine, doth tell
That at the time when first our souls are framed,
Ere in these mansions blind they come to dwell,
They live bright rays of that eternal light,
And others see, know, love, in heaven's great height,
Not toiled with aught to reason doth rebel.
Most true it is, for straight at the first sight
My mind me told that in some other place
It elsewhere saw the idea of that face,
And loved a love of heavenly pure delight.
 No wonder now I feel so fair a flame,
 Sith I her loved ere on this earth she came.

SONNET.

SLEEP, Silence' child, sweet father of soft rest,
Prince, whose approach peace to all mortals brings,
Indifferent host to shepherds and to kings,
Sole comforter of minds with grief opprest!
Lo, by thy charming rod all breathing things
Lie slumb'ring, with forgetfulness possest,
And yet o'er me to spread thy drowsy wings
Thou spares, alas! who cannot be thy guest.
Since I am thine, O come, but with that face
To inward light which thou are wont to show,
With feignèd solace ease a true-felt woe;
Or if, deaf god, thou do deny that grace,
　Come as thou wilt, and what thou wilt bequeath,
　I long to kiss the image of my death.

SONNET.

Ah! burning thoughts, now let me take some rest,
And your tumultuous broils a while appease;
Is 't not enough, stars, fortune, love molest
Me all at once, but ye must too displease?
Let hope, though false, yet lodge within my breast,
My high attempt, though dangerous, yet praise.
What though I trace not right heaven's steepy ways?
It doth suffice, my fall shall make me blest.
I do not doat on days, nor fear not death—
So that my life be brave, what though not long?
Let me renown'd live from the vulgar throng,
And when ye list, Heavens! take this borrowed
    breath.
  Men but like visions are, time all doth claim:
He lives who dies to win a lasting name.

SONNET.

With flaming horns the Bull now brings the year;
Melt do the horrid mountains' helms of snow;
The silver floods in pearly channels flow;
The late-bare woods green anademes do wear;
The nightingale, forgetting winter's woe,
Calls up the lazy morn her notes to hear;
Those flowers are spread which names of princes bear,
Some red, some azure, white, and golden grow;
Here lows a heifer, there bewailing strays
A harmless lamb, not far a stag rebounds;
The shepherds sing to grazing flocks sweet lays,
And all about the echoing air resounds.
　　Hills, dales, woods, floods, and everything doth
　　　　change,
　　But she in rigour, I in love am strange.

MADRIGAL.

LIKE the Idalian queen,
Her hair about her eyne,
With neck and breast's ripe apples to be seen,
At first glance of the morn,
In Cyprus' gardens gathering those fair flowers
Which of her blood were born,
I saw, but fainting saw, my paramour's.
The Graces naked danced about the place,
The winds and trees amazed
With silence on her gazed;
The flowers did smile, like those upon her face;
And as their aspen stalks those fingers band,
That she might read my case,
A hyacinth I wished me in her hand.

SONNET.

Trust not, sweet soul, those curled waves of gold,
With gentle tides, which on your temples flow,
Nor temples spread with flakes of virgin snow,
Nor snow of cheeks with Tyrian grain enrolled.
Trust not those shining lights which wrought my woe,
When first I did their burning rays behold,
Nor voice, whose sounds more strange effects do show
Than of the Thracian harper have been told.
Look to this dying lily, fading rose,
Dark hyacinth, of late whose blushing beams
Made all the neighbouring herbs and grass rejoice,
And think how little is 'twixt life's extremes.
   The cruel tyrant that did kill those flowers,
   Shall once, ah me! not spare that spring of yours.

SONNET.

IF crost with all mishaps be my poor life,
If one short day I never spent in mirth,
If my sp'rit with itself holds lasting strife,
If sorrow's death is but new sorrow's birth ;
If this vain world be but a sable stage
Where slave-born man plays to the scoffing stars ;
If youth be toss'd with love, with weakness age,
If knowledge serve to hold our thoughts in wars ;
If Time can close the hundred mouths of Fame,
And make, what long since past, like that to be ;
If virtue only be an idle name,
If I, when I was born, was born to die ;
  Why seek I to prolong these loathsome days?
  The fairest rose in shortest time decays.

SONNET.

THE sun is fair when he, with crimson crown
And flaming rubies, leaves his eastern bed;
Fair is Thaumantius, in her crystal gown,
When clouds, engemm'd, hang azure, green, and red:
To western worlds when wearied day goes down,
And from Heaven's windows each star shows her
    head,
Earth's silent daughter, Night, is fair, though brown;
Fair is the moon, though in love's livery clad;
Fair Chloris is when she doth paint April;
Fair are the meads, the woods; the floods are fair;
Fair looketh Ceres with her yellow hair,
And apples' queen when, rose-cheeked, she doth smile.
    That heaven, and earth, and seas are fair is true,
    Yet true that all not please so much as you.

SONNET.

Ah! who can see those fruits of Paradise,
Celestial cherries, which so sweetly swell,
That sweetness' self confined there seems to dwell,
And all those sweetest parts about despise?
Ah! who can see and feel no flame surprise
His hardened heart? For me, alas! too well
I know their force, and how they do excel.
Now burn I through desire, now do I freeze;
I die, dear life, unless to me be given
As many kisses as the spring hath flowers,
Or as the silver drops of Iris' showers,
Or as the stars in all-embracing heaven;
  And if, displeased, ye of the match complain,
  Ye shall have leave to take them back again.

SONNET.

Dear wood, and you, sweet solitary place,
Where from the vulgar I estrangèd live,
Contented more with what your shades me give
Than if I had what Thetis doth embrace;
What snaky eye, grown jealous of my peace,
Now from your silent horrors would me drive,
When sun, progressing in his glorious race
Beyond the Twins, doth near our pole arrive?
What sweet delight a quiet life affords,
And what is it to be of bondage free,
Far from the madding worldling's hoarse discords,
Sweet flowery place, I first did learn of thee.
　　Ah! if I were mine own, your dear resorts
　　I would not change with princes' stately courts.

SEXTAIN.

SITH gone is my delight and only pleasure,
The last of all my hopes, the cheerful sun
That cleared my life's dark day, nature's sweet
    treasure,
More dear to me than all beneath the moon,
What resteth now, but that upon this mountain
I weep, till Heaven transform me in a fountain

Fresh, fair, delicious, crystal, pearly fountain,
On whose smooth face to look she oft took pleasure,
Tell me (so may thy streams long cheer this mountain,
So serpent ne'er thee stain, nor scorch thee sun,
So may with gentle beams thee kiss the moon),
Dost thou not mourn to want so fair a treasure?

While she her glassed in thee, rich Tagus' treasure
Thou envy needed not, nor yet the fountain
In which that hunter saw the naked moon;
Absence hath robbed thee of thy wealth and pleasure,
And I remain like marigold of sun
Deprived, that dies by shadow of some mountain.

Nymphs of the forests, nymphs who on this mountain
Are wont to dance, showing your beauty's treasure
To goat-feet Sylvans and the wond'ring sun,
When, as you gather flowers about this fountain,
Bid her farewell who placèd here her pleasure,
And sing her praises to the stars and moon.

Among the lesser lights as is the moon,
Blushing through scarf of clouds on Latmos' moun-
     tain,
Or when her silver locks she looks for pleasure
In Thetis' streams, proud of so gay a treasure,
Such was my fair when she sat by this fountain
With other nymphs, to shun the amorous sun.

As is our earth in absence of the sun,
Or when of sun deprivèd is the moon ;
As is without a verdant shade a fountain,
Or wanting grass, a mead, a vale, a mountain ;
Such is my state, bereft of my dear treasure,
To know whose only worth was all my pleasure.

Ne'er think of pleasure, heart ; eyes, shun the sun ;
Tears be your treasure, which the wand'ring moon
Shall see you shed by mountain, vale, and fountain.

MADRIGAL.

THE ivory, coral, gold,
Of breast, of lips, of hair,
So lively Sleep doth show to inward sight,
That, wake, I think I hold
No shadow but my fair.
Myself so to deceive,
With long-shut eyes I shun the irksome light.
Such pleasure thus I have,
Delighting in false gleams,
If Death Sleep's brother be,
   And souls relieved of sense have so sweet dreams,
   That I would wish me thus to dream and die.

SONNET.

PLACE me where angry Titan burns the Moor,
And thirsty Afric fiery monsters brings,
Or where the new-born phœnix spreads her wings,
And troops of wond'ring birds her flight adore;
Place me by Gange, or Ind's empampered shore,
Where smiling heavens on earth cause double springs;
Place me where Neptune's quire of syrens sings,
Or where, made hoarse through cold, he leaves to
    roar;
Me place where Fortune doth her darlings crown,
A wonder or a spark in Envy's eye,
Or late outrageous fates upon me frown,
And pity wailing see disaster'd me;
  Affection's print my mind so deep doth prove,
  I may forget myself, but not my love.

POEMS:

AMOROUS, FUNERAL, DIVINE.

SECOND PART.

SONNET.

SWEET soul, which in the April of thy years
So to enrich the heaven mad'st poor this round,
And now with golden rays of glory crowned
Most blest abid'st above the sphere of spheres
If heavenly laws, alas! have not thee bound
From looking to this globe that all upbears,
If ruth and pity there above be found,
O deign to lend a look unto those tears.
Do not disdain, dear ghost, this sacrifice,
And though I raise not pillars to thy praise,
Mine offerings take; let this for me suffice,
My heart a living pyramid I raise;
   And whilst kings' tombs with laurels flourish green,
   Thine shall with myrtles and these flowers be seen.

MADRIGAL.

THIS life, which seems so fair,
Is like a bubble blown up in the air,
By sporting children's breath,
Who chase it everywhere,
  And strive who can most motion it bequeath :
And though it sometime seem of its own might,
Like to an eye of gold, to be fixed there,
And firm to hover in that empty height,
That only is because it is so light.
But in that pomp it doth not long appear :
  For even when most admired, it in a thought,
  As swelled from nothing, doth dissolve in nought.

SONG.

O PAN, Pan, winter is fallen in our May,
Turned is in night our day!
Forsake thy pipe, a sceptre take to thee,
Thy locks dis-garland, thou black Jove shalt be.
Thy flocks do leave the meads,
And, loathing three-leaved grass, hold up their heads;
The streams not glide now with a gentle roar,
Nor birds sing as before;
Hills stand with clouds, like mourners, veiled in black,
And owls on cabin roofs foretell our wrack.
    That zephyr every year
So soon was heard to sigh in forests here,
It was for her: that wrapt in gowns of green,
Meads were so early seen,
That in the saddest months oft sung the merles,
It was for her; for her trees dropped forth pearls.
That proud and stately courts
Did envy those our shades, and calm resorts,
It was for her; and she is gone, O woe!
Woods cut again do grow,
Bud doth the rose and daisy, winter done,
But we, once dead, no more do see the sun.
    Whose name shall now make ring
The echoes? of whom shall the nymphets sing?

Whose heavenly voice, whose soul-invading strains,
Shall fill with joy the plains?
What hair, what eyes, can make the morn in east
Weep, that a fairer riseth in the west?
Fair sun, post still away,
No music here is found thy course to stay.
Sweet Hybla swarms, with wormwood fill your bowers,
Gone is the flower of flowers.
Blush no more, rose, nor, lily, pale remain,
Dead is that beauty which yours late did stain.
     Ah me! to wail my plight
Why have not I as many eyes as night
Or as that shepherd which Jove's love did keep,
That I still still may weep?
But though I had, my tears unto my cross
Were not yet equal, nor grief to my loss.
Yet of your briny showers,
Which I here pour, may spring as many flowers
As came of those which fell from Helen's eyes;
And when ye do arise,
May every leaf in sable letters bear
The doleful cause for which ye spring up here.

SONNET.

SWEET Spring, thou turn'st with all thy goodly train,
Thy head with flames, thy mantle bright with flowers;
The zephyrs curl the green locks of the plain,
The clouds for joy in pearls weep down their showers.
Thou turn'st, sweet youth, but, ah! my pleasant hours
And happy days with thee come not again;
The sad memorials only of my pain
Do with thee turn, which turn my sweets in sours.
Thou art the same which still thou wast before,
Delicious, wanton, amiable, fair;
But she, whose breath embalmed thy wholesome air,
Is gone, nor gold nor gems her can restore.
    Neglected Virtue, seasons go and come,
    While thine, forgot, lie closèd in a tomb.

SONNET.

WHAT doth it serve to see Sun's burning face,
And skies enamell'd with both the Indies' gold?
Or moon at night in jetty chariot rolled,
And all the glory of that starry place?
What doth it serve earth's beauty to behold,
The mountain's pride, the meadow's flowery grace,
The stately comeliness of forests old,
The sport of floods, which would themselves embrace?
What doth it serve to hear the Sylvans' songs,
The wanton merle, the nightingale's sad strains,
Which in dark shades seem to deplore my wrongs?
For what doth serve all that this world contains,
   Sith she for whom those once to me were dear,
   No part of them can have now with me here?

SONNET.

As, in a dusky and tempestuous night,
A star is wont to spread her locks of gold,
And while her pleasant rays abroad are rolled,
Some spiteful cloud doth rob us of her sight :
Fair soul, in this black age so shined thou bright,
And made all eyes with wonder thee behold.
Till ugly Death, depriving us of light,
In his grim misty arms thee did enfold.
Who more shall vaunt true beauty here to see?
What hope doth more in any heart remain,
That such perfections shall his reason reign,
If beauty, with thee born, too, died with thee?
World, plain no more of Love, nor count his
harms ;
With his pale trophies Death hath hung his arms.

N   V

SONG.

It autumn was, and on our hemisphere
Fair Ericyne began bright to appear;
Night westward did her gemmy world decline,
And hide her lights, that greater light might shine;
The crested bird had given alarum twice
To lazy mortals, to unlock their eyes;
The owl had left to plain, and from each thorn
The winged musicians did salute the morn,
Who, while she glassed her locks in Ganges' streams,
Set open wide the crystal port of dreams;
When I, whose eyes no drowsy night could close,
In sleep's soft arms did quietly repose,
And, for that heavens to die me did deny,
Death's image kissèd, and as dead did lie.
I lay as dead, but scarce charmed were my cares,
And slakèd scarce my sighs, scarce dried my tears,
Sleep scarce the ugly figures of the day
Had with his sable pencil put away,
And left me in a still and calmy mood,
When by my bed methought a virgin stood,
A virgin in the blooming of her prime,
If such rare beauty measured be by time.
Her head a garland wore of opals bright,

About her flowed a gown as pure as light,
Dear amber locks gave umbrage to her face,
Where modesty high majesty did grace ;
Her eyes such beams sent forth that but with pain
Here weaker sights their sparkling could sustain.
No deity feigned, which haunts the silent woods,
Is like to her, nor syren of the floods.
Such is the golden planet of the year,
When, blushing in the east, he doth appear.
Her grace did beauty, voice yet grace did pass,
Which thus through pearls and rubies broken was.

"How long wilt thou," said she, "estranged from joy,
Paint shadows to thyself of false annoy?
How long thy mind with horrid shapes affright,
And in imaginary ills delight,
Esteem that loss which, well when viewed, is gain,
Or if a loss, yet not a loss to plain?
O leave thy tirèd soul more to molest,
And think that woe when shortest then is best.
If she for whom thou deaf'nest thus the sky
Be dead, what then? was she not born to die?
Was she not mortal born? If thou dost grieve
That times should be in which she should not live,
Ere e'er she was weep that day's wheel was rolled,
Weep that she lived not in the age of gold ;
For that she was not then, thou may'st deplore
As duly as that now she is no more.
If only she had died, thou sure hadst cause
To blame the destinies, and heaven's iron laws :
But look how many millions her advance,
What numbers with her enter in this dance,

With those which are to come: shall heavens them
    stay,
And all fair order break, thee to obey?
Even as thy birth, death, which doth thee appal,
A piece is of the life of this great all.
Strong cities die, die do high palmy reigns,
And, weakling, thou thus to be handled plains.
    "If she be dead, then she of loathsome days
Hath past the line, whose length but loss bewrays;
Then she hath left this filthy stage of care,
Where pleasure seldom, woe doth still repair.
For all the pleasures which it doth contain,
Not countervail the smallest minute's pain.
And tell me, thou who dost so much admire
This little vapour, smoke, this spark, or fire,
Which life is called, what doth it thee bequeath
But some few years which birth draws out to death?
Which if thou paragon with lustres run,
And them whose career is but now begun,
In day's great vast they shall far less appear
Than with the sea when matchèd is a tear.
But why wouldst thou here longer wish to be?
One year doth serve all nature's pomp to see,
Nay, even one day and night: this moon, that sun,
Those lesser fires about this round which run,
Be but the same which, under Saturn's reign,
Did the serpenting seasons interchain.
How oft doth life grow less by living long?
And what excelleth but what dieth young?
For age, which all abhor, yet would embrace,
Whiles makes the mind as wrinkled as the face;

And when that destinies conspire with worth,
That years not glory wrong, life soon goes forth.
Leave then laments, and think thou didst not live,
Laws to that first Eternal Cause to give,
But to obey those laws which he hath given,
And bow unto the just decrees of Heaven,
Which cannot err, whatever foggy mists
Do blind men in these sublunary lists.
   " But what if she for whom thou spend'st those
      groans,
And wastest life's dear torch in ruthful moans,
She for whose sake thou hat'st the joyful light,
Court'st solitary shades, and irksome night,
Doth live? O! if thou canst, through tears, a space
Lift thy dimm'd lights, and look upon this face,
Look if those eyes which, fool, thou didst adore,
Shine not more bright than they were wont before ;
Look if those roses death could aught impair,
Those roses to thee once which seemed so fair ;
And if those locks have lost aught of that gold
Which erst they had when thou them didst behold.
I live, and happy live, but thou art dead,
And still shalt be, till thou be like me made.
Alas! while we are wrapt in gowns of earth,
And blind, here suck the air of woe beneath,
Each thing in sense's balances we weigh,
And but with toil and pain the truth descry.
   " Above this vast and admirable frame,
This temple visible, which world we name,
Within whose walls so many lamps do burn,
So many arches opposite do turn,

Where elemental brethren nurse their strife,
And by intestine wars maintain their life,
There is a world, a world of perfect bliss.
Pure, immaterial, bright, more far from this
Than that high circle, which the rest enspheres,
Is from this dull ignoble vale of tears;
A world, where all is found, that here is found,
But further discrepant than heaven and ground.
It hath an earth, as hath this world of yours,
With creatures peopled, stored with trees and flowers;
It hath a sea, like sapphire girdle cast,
Which decketh of harmonious shores the waste:
It hath pure fire, it hath delicious air,
Moon, sun, and stars, heavens wonderfully fair:
But there flowers do not fade, trees grow not old,
The creatures do not die through heat nor cold;
Sea there not tossèd is, nor air made black,
Fire doth not nurse itself on others' wrack;
There heavens be not constrained about to range,
For this world hath no need of any change:
The minutes grow not hours, hours rise not days,
Days make no months but ever-blooming Mays.
    "Here I remain, but hitherward do tend
All who their span of days in virtue spend:
Whatever pleasure this low place contains,
It is a glance but of what high remains.
Those who, perchance, think there can nothing be
Without this wide expansion which they see,
And that nought else mounts stars' circumference,
For that nought else is subject to their sense,
Feel such a case; as one whom some abysm

Of the deep ocean kept had all his time,
Who, born and nourished there, can scarcely dream
That ought can live without that briny stream,
Cannot believe that there be temples, towers,
That go beyond his caves and dampish bowers,
Or there be other people, manners, laws,
Than them he finds within the roaring waves —
That sweeter flowers do spring than grow on rocks,
Or beasts be which excel the scaly flocks—
That other elements be to be found
Than is the water, and this ball of ground.
But think that man from those abysms were brought,
And saw what curious nature here hath wrought,
Did see the meads, the tall and shady woods,
The hills did see, the clear and ambling floods,
The diverse shapes of beasts which kinds forth bring,
The feathered troops, that fly and sweetly sing,
Did see the palaces, the cities fair,
The form of human life, the fire, the air,
The brightness of the sun that dims his sight,
The moon, the ghastly splendours of the night:
What uncouth rapture would his mind surprise!
How would he his late-dear resort despise!
How would he muse how foolish he had been
To think nought be, but what he there had seen!
    "Why did we get this high and vast desire
Unto immortal things still to aspire?
Why doth our mind extend it beyond time,
And to that highest happiness even climb,
If we be nought but what to sense we seem,
And dust, as most of worldlings us esteem?

We be not made for earth, though here we come,
More than the embryon for the mother's womb;
It weeps to be made free, and we complain
To leave this loathsome jail of care and pain.

"But thou who vulgar footsteps dost not trace,
Learn to raise up thy mind unto this place,
And what earth-creeping mortals most affect,
If not at all to scorn, yet to neglect:
O chase not shadows vain, which, when obtained,
Were better lost than with such travail gained.
Think that on earth, which humans greatness call,
Is but a glorious title to live thrall;
That sceptres, diadems, and chairs of state,
Not in themselves, but to small minds are great;
How those who loftiest mount do hardest light,
And deepest falls be from the highest height;
How fame an echo is, how all renown
Like to a blasted rose, ere night falls down :
And though it something were, think how this round
Is but a little point, which doth it bound.

"O leave that love which reacheth but to dust,
And in that love eternal only trust,
And beauty, which, when once it is possest,
Can only fill the soul, and make it blest.
Pale envy, jealous emulations, fears,
Sighs, plaints, remorse, here have no place, nor tears,
False joys, vain hopes, here be not hate nor wrath;
What ends all love, here most augments it, death.
If such force had the dim glance of an eye,
Which some few days thereafter was to die,
That it could make thee leave all other things,

And like the taper-fly there burn thy wings;
And if a voice, of late which could but wail,
Such pow'r had, as through ears thy soul to steal:
If once thou on that only fair couldst gaze,
What flames of love would he within thee raise?
In what amazing maze would it thee bring,
To hear but once that quire celestial sing?
The fairest shapes on which thy love did seize,
Which erst did breed delight, then would displease,
Then discords hoarse were earth's enticing sounds,
All music but a noise which sense confounds.
This great and burning glass that clears all eyes,
And musters with such glory in the skies;
That silver star which with its sober light
Makes day oft envy the eye-pleasing night:
Those golden letters which so brightly shine
In heaven's great volume gorgeously divine;
The wonders all in sea, in earth, in air,
Be but dark pictures of that sovereign Fair—
Be tongues, which still thus cry unto your ear,
Could ye amidst worlds' cataracts them hear.
  "From fading things, fond wights, lift your desire,
And in our beauty, his, us made, admire.
If we seem fair, O think, how fair is he
Of whose fair fairness shadows, steps, we be.
No shadow can compare it with the face,
No step with that dear foot that did it trace.
Your souls immortal are, then place them hence,
And do not drown them in the must of sense,
Do not, O do not, by false pleasures' might
Deprive them of that true and sole delight.

That happiness ye seek is not below;
Earth's sweetest joy is but disguisèd woe."
    Here did she pause, and with a mild aspect
Did towards me those lamping twins direct;
The wonted rays I knew, and thrice essayed
To answer make, thrice falt'ring tongue it stayed;
And while upon that face I fed my sight,
Methought she vanished up in Titan's light,
Who gilding with his rays each hill and plain,
Seemed to have brought the goldsmith's world again

TEARS ON THE DEATH OF MŒLIADES.

CHASTE maids which haunt fair Aganippe's well,
And you in Tempe's sacred shade who dwell,
Let fall your harps, cease tunes of joy to sing,
Dishevellèd make all Parnassus ring
With anthems sad ! thy music, Phœbus, turn
In doleful plaints, whilst joy itself doth mourn !
Dead is thy darling who decor'd thy bays,
Who oft was wont to cherish thy sweet lays,
And to a trumpet raise thine amorous style,
That floating Delos envy might this isle.
You, Acidalian archers, break your bows,
Your brandons quench, with tears blot beauty's
    snows,
And bid your weeping mother yet again
A second Adon's death, nay Mars's plain.
His eyes once were your darts, nay, even his name,
Wherever heard, did every heart inflame :
Tagus did court his love with golden streams,
Rhine with his towns, fair Seine with all she claims.
But ah ! poor lovers, death did them betray,
And, not suspected, made their hopes his prey.

Tagus bewails his loss with golden streams,
Rhine with his towns, fair Seine with all she claims.
Mœliades sweet courtly nymphs deplore,
From Thule to Hydaspes' pearly shore.

Delicious meads, whose checker'd plain forth brings
White, golden, azure flowers, which once were kings,
In mourning black their shining colours dye,
Bow down their heads, whilst sighing zephyrs fly.
Queen of the fields, whose blush makes blush the
morn,
Sweet rose, a prince's death in purple mourn :
O hyacinths, for aye your AI keep still,
Nay, with more marks of woe, your leaves now fill ;
And you, O flower of Helen's tears first born,
Into those liquid pearls again you turn :
Your green locks, forests, cut, in weeping myrrhs,
The deadly cypress, and ink-dropping firs,
Your palms and myrtles change; from shadows dark
Winged syrens wail : and you, sad echoes, mark
The lamentable accents of their moan,
And plain that brave Mœliades is gone.
Stay, sky, thy turning course, and now become
A stately arch, unto the earth his tomb ;
Over which aye the watery Iris keep,
And sad Electra's sisters which still weep.
Mœliades sweet courtly nymphs deplore,
From Thule to Hydaspes' pearly shore.

Dear ghost, forgive these our untimely tears,
By which our loving mind, though weak, appears.
Our loss, not thine, when we complain, we weep ;
For thee the glist'ring walls of heaven do keep

Beyond the planets' wheels, above that source
Of spheres that turns the lower in its course,
Where sun doth never set, nor ugly night
Ever appears in mourning garments dight,
Where Boreas' stormy trumpet doth not sound,
Nor clouds, in lightnings bursting, minds astound,
From care's cold climates far, and hot desire,
Where time is banished, ages ne'er expire.
Amongst pure sp'rits environèd with beams,
Thou think'st all things below to be but dreams,
And joy'st to look down to the azured bars
Of heaven, indented all with streaming stars.
And in their turning temples to behold,
In silver robe the moon, the sun in gold,
Like young eye-speaking lovers in a dance,
With majesty by turns retire, advance.
Thou wond'rest earth to see hang like a ball,
Closed in the ghastly cloister of this all,
And that poor men should prove so madly fond,
To toss themselves for a small foot of ground,
Nay, that they even dare brave the powers above,
From this base stage of change that cannot move.
All worldly pomp and pride thou seest arise
Like smoke, that scatt'reth in the empty skies.
Other hills and forests, other sumptuous towers,
Amazed thou find'st, excelling our poor bowers ;
Courts void of flattery, of malice minds,
Pleasure which lasts, not such as reason blinds.
Far sweeter songs thou hear'st, and carollings,
Whilst heavens do dance, and quire of angels sings,
Than mouldy minds could feign. Even our annoy,

If it approach that place, is chang'd in joy.

Rest blessed sp'rit, rest satiate with the sight
Of him whose beams both dazzle and delight,
Life of all lives, cause of each other cause,
The sphere and centre where the mind doth pause ;
Narcissus of himself, himself the well,
Lover, and beauty, that doth all excel.
Rest, happy ghost, and wonder in that glass
Where seen is all that shall be, is, or was,
While shall be, is, or was do pass away,
And nought remain but an eternal day.
For ever rest ; thy praise fame may enroll
In golden annals, whilst about the pole
The slow Boötes turns, or sun doth rise
With scarlet scarf, to cheer the mourning skies.
The virgins to thy tomb may garlands bear
Of flowers, and on each flower let fall a tear ;
Mœliades sweet courtly nymphs deplore,
From Thule to Hydaspes' pearly shore.

URANIA, OR SPIRITUAL POEMS.

THRICE happy he, who by some shady grove,
Far from the clamorous world doth live his own,
Though solitary, who is not alone,
But doth converse with that eternal love.
O how more sweet is birds' harmonious moan,
Or the soft sobbings of the widowed dove,
Than those smooth whisp'rings near a prince's throne,
Which good make doubtful, do the evil approve!
O how more sweet is zephyr's wholesome breath,
And sighs perfumed, which new-born flowers unfold,
Than that applause vain honour doth bequeath!
How sweet are streams to poison drunk in gold!
  The world is full of horrors, falsehoods, slights:
  Woods' silent shades have only true delights.

———

WHY, wordlings, do ye trust frail honour's dreams,
And lean to gilded glories which decay?
Why do ye toil to registrate your names
On icy columns, which soon melt away?
True honour is not here; that place it claims,
Were black-brow'd night doth not exile the day,

Nor no far-shining lamp dives in the sea,
But an eternal sun spreads lasting beams.
There it attendeth you, where spotless bands
Of sp'rits stand gazing on their sovereign bliss,
Where years not hold it in their cank'ring hands,
But who, once noble, ever noble is.

    Look home, lest he your weakened wit make thrall,
Who Eden's foolish gardener erst made fall.

EPIGRAM.

OF PHILLIS.

IN petticoat of green,
Her hair about her eyne,
Phillis beneath an oak
Sat milking her fair flock :
Among that strained moisture, rare delight !
Her hand seem'd milk in milk, it was so white.

FORTH FEASTING.

WHAT blust'ring noise now interrupts my sleep?
What echoing shouts thus cleave my crystal deep,
And call me hence from out my watery court?
What melody, what sounds of joy and sport,
Be these here hurled from every neighbour spring?
With what loud rumours do the mountains ring,
Which in unusual pomp on tip-toes stand,
And, full of wonder, overlook the land?
Whence come these glitt'ring throngs, these meteors
      bright,
This golden people set unto my sight?
Whence doth this praise, applause, and love arise?
What load-star eastward draweth thus all eyes?
And do I wake, or have some dreams conspired
To mock my sense with shadows much desired?
Stare I that living face, see I those looks,
Which with delight wont to amaze my brooks?
Do I behold that worth, that man divine,
This age's glory, by these banks of mine?
Then is it true, what long I wished in vain,
That my much-loving prince is come again?
So unto them whose zenith is the pole,
When six black months are past, the sun doth roll;

O   V

So after tempest to sea-tossèd wights
Fair Helen's brothers show their cheering lights;
So comes Arabia's marvel from her woods,
And far, far off is seen by Memphis' floods,
The feathered sylvans, cloud-like, by her fly,
And with applauding clangours beat the sky,
Nile wonders, Serap's priests entrancèd rave,
And in Mygdonian stone her shape engrave,
In golden leaves write down the joyful time
In which Apollo's bird came to their clime.

Let mother earth now deckt with flowers be seen,
And sweet-breath'd zephyrs curl the meadows green.
Let heavens weep rubies in a crimson shower
Such as on Indias' shores they use to pour,
Or with that golden storm the fields adorn,
Which Jove rained when his blue-eyed maid was born.
May never hours the web of day out-weave,
May never night rise from her sable cave.
Swell proud, my billows, faint not to declare
Your joys as ample as their causes are;
For murmurs hoarse sound like Arion's harp,
Now delicately flat, now sweetly sharp;
And you, my nymphs, rise from your moist repair,
Strew all your springs and grots with lilies fair.
Some swiftest-footed, get them hence, and pray
Our floods and lakes come keep this holiday;
Whate'er beneath Albania's hills do run,
Which see the rising or the setting sun,
Which drink stern Grampius' mists, or Ochels' snows;
Stone-rolling Tay, Tyne tortoise-like that flows,
The pearly Don, the Dees, the fertile Spey,

Wild Neverne which doth see our longest day,
Ness smoking sulphur, Leave with mountains crowned,
Strange Lomond for his floating isles renowned,
The Irish Rian, Ken, the silver Ayr,
The snaky Dun, the Ore with rushy hair,
The crystal-streaming Nid, loud-bellowing Clyde,
Tweed, which no more our kingdoms shall divide,
Rank-swelling Annan, Lid with curled streams,
The Esks, the Solway, where they lose their names—
To ev'ry one proclaim our joys and feasts,
Our triumphs; bid all come, and be our guests;
And as they meet in Neptune's azure hall,
Bid them bid sea-gods keep this festival.
This day shall by our currents be renowned,
Our hills about shall still this day resound:
Nay, that our love more to this day appear,
Let us with it henceforth begin our year.
    To virgins flowers, to sun-burnt earth the rain,
To mariners fair winds amidst the main,
Cool shades to pilgrims which hot glances burn,
Please not so much to us as thy return.
That day, dear Prince, which reft us of thy sight,
Day, no, but darkness, and a cloudy night,
Did freight our breast with sighs, our eyes with tears,
Turned minutes in sad months, sad months in years;
Trees left to flourish, meadows to bear flowers,
Brooks hid their heads within their sedgy bowers;
Fair Ceres cursed our fields with barren frost,
As if again she had her daughter lost;
The Muses left our groves, and for sweet songs
Sat sadly silent, or did weep their wrongs.

Ye know it, meads, ye murmuring woods, it know,
Hills, dales, and caves, copartners of their woe;
And ye it know, my streams, which from their eyne
Oft on your glass received their pearled brine.
O Naïads dear, said they, Napæas fair,
O nymphs of trees, nymphs which on hills repair,
Gone are those maiden glories, gone that state,
Which made all eyes admire our hap of late.
As looks the heaven when never star appears,
But slow and weary shroud them in their spheres,
While Tithon's wife embosom'd by him lies,
And world doth languish in a dreary guise—
As looks a garden of its beauty spoiled—
As wood in winter by rough Boreas soiled —
As portraits razed of colours use to be—
So looked these abject bounds deprived of thee.
  While as my rills enjoyed thy royal gleams,
They did not envy Tiber's haughty streams,
Nor wealthy Tagus with his golden ore,
Nor clear Hydaspes, which on pearls doth roar,
Empamper'd Gange, that sees the sun new-born,
Nor Acheloüs with his flowery horn,
Nor floods which near Elysian fields do fall.
For why?—thy sight did serve to them for all.
No place there is so desert, so alone,
Even from the frozen to the torrid zone,
From flaming Hecla to great Quincy's Lake,
Which thine abode could not most happy make.
All those perfections which by bounteous Heaven
To diverse worlds in diverse times were given,
The starry senate poured at once on thee,

That thou exemplar might'st to others be.
　Thy life was kept till the three sisters spun
Their threads of gold, and then it was begun.
With curled clouds when skies do look most fair,
And no disordered blasts disturb the air,
When lilies do them deck in azure gowns,
And new-born roses blush with golden crowns,
To bode how calm we under thee should live,
What halcyonean days thy reign should give,
And to two flowery diadems thy right,
The heavens thee made a partner of the light.
Scarce wast thou born, when, joined in friendly bands,
Two mortal foes with other claspèd hands.
With virtue fortune strove which most should grace
Thy place for thee, thee for so high a place :
One vowed thy sacred breast not to forsake,
The other on thee not to turn her back,
And that thou more her love's effect might'st feel,
For thee she rent her sail, and broke her wheel.
　When years thee vigour gave, O then how clear
Did smothered sparkles in bright flames appear !
Amongst the woods to force a flying hart,
To pierce the mountain wolf with feathered dart,
See falcons climb the clouds, the fox ensnare,
Outrun the wind-outrunning dædal hare,
To loose a trampling steed alongst a plain,
And in meand'ring gyres him bring again,
The press thee making place, were vulgar things :
In admiration's air, on glory's wings,
O ! thou far from the common pitch didst rise,
With thy designs to dazzle envy's eyes.

Thou sought'st to know this all's eternal source,
Of ever-turning heavens the restless course,
Their fixèd eyes, their lights which wand'ring run,
Whence moon her silver hath, his gold the sun,
If destine be or no, if planets can
By fierce aspects force the free-will of man.
The light and spiring fire, the liquid air,
The flaming dragons, comets with red hair,
Heaven's tilting lance, artillery, and bow,
Loud-sounding trumpets, darts of hail and snow,
The roaring element with people dumb,
The earth, with what conceived is in her womb,
What on her moves, were set unto thy sight,
Till thou didst find their causes, essence, might.
But unto nought thou so thy mind didst strain,
As to be read in man, and learn to reign,
To know the weight and Atlas of a crown,
To spare the humble, proudlings pester down.
When from those piercing cares which thrones invest,
As thorns the rose, thou wearied wouldst thee rest,
With lute in hand, full of celestial fire,
To the Pierian groves thou didst retire.
There, garlanded with all Urania's flowers,
In sweeter lays than builded Thebes' towers,
Or them which charmed the dolphins in the main,
Or which did call Eurydice again,
Thou sung'st away the hours, till from their sphere
Stars seemed to shoot, thy melody to hear.
The god with golden hair, the sister maids,
Left nymphal Helicon, their Tempe's shades,
To see thine isle, here lost their native tongue,

And in thy world-divided language sung.

Who of thine after-age can count the deeds,
With all that fame in time's huge annals reads?
How by example more than any law
This people fierce thou didst to goodness draw,
How, while the neighbour worlds, tous'd by the Fates,
So many Phaëtons had in their states,
Which turned in heedless flames their burnished
    thrones,
Thou, as ensphered, keep'dst temperate thy zones.
In Afric shores the sands that ebb and flow,
The speckled flowers in unshorn meads that grow,
He sure may count, with all the waves that meet
To wash the Mauritanian Atlas' feet.
Though thou were not a crownèd king by birth,
Thy worth deserves the richest crown on earth.
Search this half-sphere and the opposite ground,
Where is such wit and bounty to be found?
As into silent night, when near the bear
The virgin huntress shines at full most clear,
And strives to match her brother's golden light,
The host of stars doth vanish in her sight,
Arcturus dies, cooled is the lion's ire,
Po burns no more with Phaëtontal fire,
Orion faints to see his arms grow black,
And that his blazing sword he now doth lack :
So Europe's lights, all bright in their degree,
Lose all their lustre paragon'd with thee.
By just descent thou from more kings dost shine
Than many can name men in all their line.
What most they toil to find, and finding hold,

Thou scornest, orient gems and flatt'ring gold ;
Esteeming treasure surer in men's breasts
Than when immured with marble, closed in chests.
No stormy passions do disturb thy mind,
No mists of greatness ever could thee blind.
Who yet hath been so meek? Thou life didst give
To them who did repine to see thee live.
What prince by goodness hath such kingdoms gained?
Who hath so long his people's peace maintained?
Their swords are turned in scythes, in coulters spears,
Some giant post their antique armour bears.
Now, where the wounded knight his life did bleed,
The wanton swain sits piping on a reed,
And where the cannon did Jove's thunder scorn,
The gaudy huntsman winds his shrill-tuned horn,
Her green locks Ceres without fear doth dye,
The pilgrim safely in the shade doth lie,
Both Pan and Pales careless keep their flocks,
Seas have no dangers save the winds and rocks.
Thou art this isle's palladium, neither can,
While thou art kept, it be o'erthrown by man.

Let others boast of blood and spoils of foes,
Fierce rapines, murders, Iliads of woes,
Of hated pomp, and trophies reared fair,
Gore-spangled ensigns streaming in the air,
Count how they make the Scythian them adore,
The Gaditan, the soldier of Aurore.
Unhappy vauntry ! to enlarge their bounds,
Which charge themselves with cares, their friends
    with wounds,
Which have no law to their ambitious will,

But, man-plagues, born are human blood to spill.
Thou a true victor art, sent from above,
What others strain by force to gain by love.
World-wand'ring fame this praise to thee imparts,
To be the only monarch of all hearts.
They many fear who are of many feared ;
And kingdoms got by wrongs by wrongs are teared,
Such thrones as blood doth raise, blood throweth
    down :
No guard so sure as love unto a crown.

Eye of our western world, Mars-daunting King,
With whose renown the earth's seven climates ring,
Thy deeds not only claim these diadems,
To which, Thame, Liffey, Tay, subject their streams,
But to thy virtues rare, and gifts, is due
All that the planets of the year doth view :
Sure, if the world above did want a prince,
The world above to it would take thee hence.

That murder, rapine, lust, are fled to hell,
And in their rooms with us the Graces dwell,
That honour more than riches men respect,
That worthiness than gold doth more effect,
That piety unmaskèd shows her face,
That innocency keeps with power her place,
That long-exiled Astrea leaves the heaven,
And useth right her sword, her weights holds even,
That the Saturnian world is come again,
Are wished effects of thy most happy reign.
That daily peace, love, truth, delights increase,
And discord, hate, fraud, with incumbers cease,
That men use strength not to shed others' blood,

But use their strength now to do other good,
That fury is enchained, disarmèd wrath,
That, save by nature's hand, there is no death,
That late grim foes like brothers other love,
That vultures prey not on the harmless dove,
That wolves with lambs do friendship entertain,
Are wished effects of thy most happy reign.
That towns increase, that ruined temples rise,
And their wind-moving vanes plant in the skies,
That ignorance and sloth hence run away,
That buried arts now rouse them to the day,
That Hyperion far beyond his bed
Doth see our lions ramp, our roses spread,
That Iber courts us, Tiber not us charms,
That Rhine with hence-brought beams his bosom
      warms,
That ill us fear, and good us do maintain,
Are wished effects of thy most happy reign.
    O virtue's pattern, glory of our times,
Sent of past days to expiate the crimes,
Great King, but better far than thou art great,
Whom state not honours, but who honours state,
By wonder born, by wonder first installed,
By wonder after to new kingdoms called,
Young, kept by wonder near home-bred alarms,
Old, saved by wonder from pale traitors' harms,
To be, for this thy reign, which wonders brings,
A king of wonders, wonder unto kings!
If Pict, Dane, Norman thy smooth yoke had seen,
Pict, Dane, and Norman had thy subjects been:
If Brutus knew the bliss thy rule doth give,

Even Brutus joy would under thee to live;
For thou thy people dost so dearly love,
That they a father, more than prince, thee prove.
   O days to be desired, age happy thrice,
If ye your heaven-sent good could duly prize!
But ye half-palsy-sick, think never right
Of what ye hold, till it be from your sight
Prize only summer's sweet and muskèd breath,
When armèd winters threaten you with death—
In pallid sickness do esteem of health,
And by sad poverty discern of wealth.
I see an age when after many years,
And revolutions of the slow-paced spheres,
These days shall be to other far esteemed,
And like Augustus' palmy reign be deemed.
The names of Arthur's fabulous paladins,
Grav'n in Time's surly brows in wrinkled lines,
Of Henrys, Edwards, famous for their fights,
Their neighbour conquests, orders new of knights,
Shall by this prince's name be past as far
As meteors are by the Idalian star.
If grey-haired Proteus' songs the truth not miss
And grey-haired Proteus oft a prophet is,
There is a land hence distant many miles,
Outreaching fiction and Atlantic isles,
Which homelings from this little world we name,
That shall emblazon with strange rites his fame,
Shall raise him statues all of purest gold,
Such as men gave unto the gods of old,
Name by him fanes, proud palaces, and towns,
With some great flood, which most their fields renowns.

This is that king who should make right each wrong
Of whom the bards and mystic sibyls sung,
The man long promised, by whose glorious reign
This isle should yet her ancient name regain,
And more of Fortunate deserve the style
Than those where heavens with double summers smile.

Run on, great Prince, thy course in glory's way,
The end the life, the evening crowns the day;
Heap worth on worth, and strongly soar above
Those heights which made the world thee first to love;
Surmount thyself, and make thine actions past
Be but as gleams or lightnings of thy last;
Let them exceed them of thy younger time,
As far as autumn doth the flowery prime.
Through this thy empire range, like world's bright eye,
That once each year surveys all earth and sky,
Now glances on the slow and resty bears,
Then turns to dry the weeping Auster's tears,
Just unto both the poles, and moveth even
In the infigured circle of the heaven.
O! long, long haunt these bounds, which by thy sight
Have now regained their former heat and light!
Here grow green woods, here silver brooks do glide,
Here meadows stretch them out with painted pride,
Embroid'ring all the banks; here hills aspire
To crown their heads with the ethereal fire;
Hills, bulwarks of our freedom, giant walls,
Which never fremdling's slight nor sword made thralls;
Each circling flood to Thetis tribute pays,
Men here, in health, outlive old Nestor's days;
Grim Saturn yet amongst our rocks remains,

Bound in our cave with many-metalled chains;
Bulls haunt our shades like Leda's lover white,
Which yet might breed Pasiphaë delight :
Our flocks fair fleeces bear, with which for sport
Endymion of old the moon did court,
High-palmèd harts amidst our forests run,
And, not impaled, the deep-mouthed hounds do shun;
The rough-foot hare him in our bushes shrouds,
And long-winged hawks do perch amidst our clouds.
The wanton wood-nymphs of the verdant spring,
Blue, golden, purple flowers shall to thee bring,
Pomona's fruits the panisks, Thetis' girls
Thy Thule's amber, with the ocean pearls :
The Tritons, herdsmen of the glassy field,
Shall give thee what far-distant shores can yield,
The Serean fleeces, Erythrean gems,
Vast Plata's silver, gold of Peru streams,
Antarctic parrots, Æthiopian plumes,
Sabæan odours, myrrh, and sweet perfumes.
And I myself, wrapt in a watchet gown,
Of reeds and lilies on my head a crown,
Shall incense to thee burn, green altars raise,
And yearly sing due pæans to thy praise.
   Ah! why should Isis only see thee shine?
Is not thy Forth as well as Isis thine?
Though Isis vaunt she hath more wealth in store,
Let it suffice thy Forth doth love thee more.
Though she for beauty may compare with Seine,
For swans and sea-nymphs with imperial Rhine,
Yet in the title may be claimed in thee,
Nor she, nor all the world, can match with me.

Now when, by honour drawn, thou shalt away
To her, already jealous of thy stay,
When in her amorous arms she doth thee fold,
And dries thy dewy hairs with hers of gold,
Much questioning of thy fare, much of thy sport,
Much of thine absence, long, howe'er so short,
And chides perhaps thy coming to the north,
Loath not to think on thy much-loving Forth.
O! love these bounds, where of thy royal stem
More than an hundred wore a diadem.
So ever gold and bays thy brows adorn,
So never time may see thy race outworn,
So of thine own still may'st thou be desired,
Of strangers feared, redoubted, and admired;
So memory thee praise, so precious hours
May character thy name in starry flowers;
So may thy high exploits at last make even
With earth thy empire, glory with the heaven.

FLOWERS OF SION.

NO TRUST IN TIME.

Look how the flower which ling'ringly doth fade,
The morning's darling late, the summer's queen,
Spoiled of that juice which kept it fresh and green,
As high as it did raise, bows low the head:
Right so my life, contentments being dead,
Or in their contraries but only seen,
With swifter speed declines than erst it spread,
And, blasted, scarce now shows what it hath been.
As doth the pilgrim therefore, whom the night
By darkness would imprison on his way,
Think on thy home, my soul, and think aright
Of what yet rests thee of life's wasting day?
    Thy sun posts westward, passèd is thy morn,
    And twice it is not given thee to be born.

HYMN OF THE ASCENSION.

BRIGHT portals of the sky,
  Embossed with sparkling stars,
Doors of eternity,
  With diamantine bars,
Your arras rich uphold,
Loose all your bolts and springs,
Ope wide your leaves of gold,
  That in your roofs may come the King of Kings.
Scarfed in a rosy cloud,
  He doth ascend the air:
Straight doth the moon him shroud
  With her resplendent hair;
The next encrystalled light
Submits to him its beams,
And he doth trace the height
  Of that fair lamp which flames of beauty's streams.

*   *   *   *   *

Now each ethereal gate
  To him hath opened been,
And glory's King in state
  His palace enters in;
Now comed is this High Priest
In the most holy place,
Not without blood addressed,
  With glory heaven, the earth to crown with grace.

Stars which all eyes were late,
   And did with wonder burn,
   His name to celebrate,
   In flaming tongues them turn ;
   Their orby crystals move
   More active than before,
   And entheate from above,
   Their sovereign prince laud, glorify, adore.
The quires of happy souls,
   Waked with that music sweet,
   Whose descant care controls,
   Their Lord in triumph meet ;
   The spotless sp'rits of light
   His trophies do extol,
   And, arched in squadrons bright,
   Greet their great Victor in his Capitol.
O glory of the heaven !
   O sole delight of earth !
   To thee all power be given,
   God's uncreated birth !
   Of mankind lover true,
   Indearer of his wrong,
   Who dost the world renew,
   Still be thou our salvation and our song !
From top of Olivet such notes did rise,
When man's Redeemer did transcend the skies !

P   V

THE WORLD A GAME.

T<small>HIS</small> world a hunting is,
The prey poor man, the Nimrod fierce is Death;
His speedy greyhounds are
Lust, sickness, envy, care,
Strife that ne'er falls amiss,
With all those ills which haunt us while we breathe.
Now, if by chance we fly
Of these the eager chase,
Old age with stealing pace
Casts up his nets, and there we panting die.

THE BLESSEDNESS OF FAITHFUL SOULS BY DEATH.

L<small>ET</small> us each day inure ourselves to die,
If this, and not our fears, be truly death,
Above the circles both of hope and faith
With fair immortal pinions to fly;
If this be death, our best part to untie,
By ruining the jail, from lust and wrath,
And every drowsy languor here beneath,
It turning deniz'd citizen of sky;
To have more knowledge than all books contain,
All pleasures even surmounting wishing power,
The fellowship of God's immortal train,
And these that time nor force shall e'er devour;
　　If this be death, what joy, what golden care
　　Of life can with death's ugliness compare!

POSTHUMOUS POEMS.

SONNET.

AH me, and I am now the man whose muse
In happier times was wont to laugh at love,
And those who suffered that blind boy abuse
The noble gifts were given them from above!
What metamorphose strange is this I prove!
Myself now scarce I find myself to be,
And think no fable Circe's tyranny,
And all the tales are told of changèd Jove.
Virtue hath taught with her philosophy
My mind unto a better cause to move.
Reason may chide her full, and oft reprove
Affection's power, but what is that to me,
　Who ever think, and never think on ought
　But that bright cherubim which thralls my thought.

LOVE VAGABONDING.

SWEET nymphs, if, as ye stray,
Ye find the froth-born goddess of the sea
All blubber'd, pale, undone,
Who seeks her giddy son,
That little god of love,
Whose golden shafts your chastest bosoms prove,
Who, leaving all the heavens, hath run away—
If ought to him that finds him she'll impart
Tell her he nightly lodgeth in my heart.

FIVE SONNETS TO GALATEA.

I.

STREPHON, in vain thou bring'st thy rhymes and songs,
Deck'd with grave Pindar's old and withered flowers;
In vain thou count'st the fair Europa's wrongs,
And her whom Jove deceived in golden showers.
Thou hast slept never under myrtles' shed,
Or, if that passion hath thy soul oppressed,
It is but for some Grecian mistress dead,
Of such old sighs thou dost discharge thy breast.
How can true love with fables hold a place?
Thou who with fables dost set forth thy love,
Thy love a pretty fable needs must prove ;
Thou suest for grace, in scorn more to disgrace.
　　I cannot think thou wert charmed by my looks,
　　O no, thou learn'dst thy love in lovers' books.

II.

No more with candid words infect mine ears,
Tell me no more how that ye pine in anguish,
When sound ye sleep; no more say that ye languish,
No more in sweet despite say you spend tears.
Who hath such hollow eyes as not to see
How those that are hair-brained boast of Apollo,
And bold give out the Muses do them follow,
Though in love's library yet no lover's he !
If we poor souls least favour but them show,
That straight in wanton lines abroad is blazed,
Their name doth soar on our fame's overthrow,
Marked is our lightness whilst their wits are praised :
　　In silent thoughts who can no secret cover,
　　He may, say we but not well, be a lover

III.

Ye who with curious numbers, sweetest art,
Frame dædal nets our beauty to surprise,
Telling strange castles builded in the skies,
And tales of Cupid's bow, and Cupid's dart;
Well howsoe'er ye act your feignèd smart,
Molesting quiet ears with tragic cries,
When you accuse our chastity's best part,
Named cruelty, ye seem not half too wise;
Yea, ye yourselves it deem most worthy praise,
Beauty's best guard, that dragon which doth keep
Hesperian fruit, the spur in you does raise
That Delian wit that otherwise may sleep:
  To cruel nymphs your lines do fame afford,
  Of many pitiful not one poor word.

IV.

If it be love to wake out all the night,
And watchful eyes drive out in dewy moans,
And when the sun brings to the world his light,
To waste the day in tears and bitter groans;
If it be love to dim weak reason's beam
With clouds of strange desire, and make the mind
In hellish agonies a heav'n to dream,
Still seeking comforts where but griefs we find;
If it be love to stain with wanton thought
A spotless chastity, and make it try
More furious flames than his whose cunning wrought
That brazen bull where he entombed did fry:
  Then sure is love the causer of such woes.
  Be you our lovers, or our mortal foes?

V.

And would you then shake off love's golden chain,
With which it is best freedom to be bound;
And cruel do you seek to heal the wound
Of love, which hath such sweet and pleasant pain?
All that is subject unto nature's reign
In skies above, or on this lower round,
When it is long and far sought, end hath found,
Doth in decadence fall, and slack remain.
Behold the moon, how gay her face doth grow
Till she kiss all the sun, then doth decay;
See how the seas tumultuously do flow
Till they embrace loved banks, then post away:
   So is 't with love; unless you love me still,
   O do not think I 'll yield unto your will.

ALL CHANGETH.

THE angry winds not aye
Do cuff the roaring deep,
And though heavens often weep,
Yet do they smile for joy when comes dismay.
Frosts do not ever kill the pleasant flowers,
And love hath sweets when gone are all the sours.
This said a shepherd, closing in his arms
His dear, who blushed to feel love's new alarms.

SONNET.

O HAIR, fair hair ! some of the golden threads
Of which love weaves the nets that passion breeds
Where me like silly bird he doth retain,
And only death can make me free again !
Ah, I you love, embrace, kiss, and adore,
For that ye shadow did that face before—
That face so full of beauty, grace, and love,
That it hath jealous made heaven's choir above.
To you I 'll tell my secret thoughts and grief,
Since she, dear she, can grant me no relief.
While me from her foul traitor absence binds,
Witness, sweet hair, with me, how love me blinds;
For when I should seek what his force restrains,
I foolish bear about his nets and chains.

MADRIGAL.

My sweet did sweetly sleep,
And on her rosy face
Stood tears of pearls, which beauty's self did weep.
I, wond'ring at her grace,
Did all amazed remain,
When Love said, "Fool, can looks thy wishes crown?
Time past comes not again."
Then did I me bow down,
    And kissing her fair breast, lips, cheeks, and eyes,
    Proved here on earth the joys of paradise.

EPITAPHS.

ON A DRUNKARD.

Nor amaranths nor roses do bequeath
Unto this hearse, but tamarisks and wine;
For that same thirst, though dead, yet doth him pine,
Which made him so carouse while he drew breath.

ARETINUS.

Here Aretino lies, most bitter gall,
Who whilst he lived spoke ill of all;
Only of God the arrant sot
Naught said, but that he knew him not.

Justice, truth, peace, and hospitality,
Friendship and love, being resolved to die,
In these lewd times, have chosen here to have
With just, true, pious, * * * their grave;
Them cherished he so much, so much did grace,
That they on earth would choose none other place.

Within the closure of this narrow grave
Lie all those graces a good wife could have;
But on this marble they shall not be read,
For then the living envy would the dead.

EPIGRAMS.

WHEN lately Pym descended into hell,
Ere he the cups of Lethe did carouse,
What place that was, he called aloud to tell;
To whom a devil, "This is the lower house."

HERE Rixus lies, a novice in the laws,
Who plains he came to hell without a cause.

OF THE ISLE OF RHE.

CHARLES, would ye quail your foes, have better luck;
Send forth some Drakes, and keep at home the
duck.*

LORD SANQUHAR.

SANQUHAR, whom this earth scarce could contain,
Having seen Italy, France, and Spain,
To finish his travels, a spectacle rare,
Was bound towards heaven, but died in the air.†

---

* In allusion to the Duke of Buckingham, and his ill-fated
expedition in the year 1627.
† Robert Crichton, Lord Sanquhar, was hanged at Westminster
on the 29th of June, 1612, for the murder of a fencing-master
named Turner.

THE
MARQUIS OF MONTROSE.

THE MARQUIS OF MONTROSE.

IF England in the age of Elizabeth produced her typical warrior-courtier-poet in the person of Sir Philip Sydney, the preux chevalier who fell at Zutphen, Scotland a few years later must be held to have produced hers in the person of the Marquis of Montrose. To the high and rare accomplishments of the Elizabethan knight, Montrose added the stronger, heroic qualities of the conqueror, the statesman, and the leader of men, and crowned his career with a martyr's devotion and death. Last and brightest star which shone on the fortunes of the ill-fated Charles I., the Great Marquis, alike by the brilliance of his achievement in the field, by his rich accomplishment and perfect chivalry, and by his high-hearted devotion to a falling cause, seems amply to deserve the title which Carlyle has given him of " the noblest of the Cavaliers."

Representative of a race which had taken a heroic part in nearly every period of Scottish history, and whose name itself is said to signify " warrior,"* James

* Graham, Graeme, or Gram is said to be derived from the old Saxon for a soldier. The name De Graham occurs in the deed *De Ecclesia de Lohworuora* of about 1150 (Reg. Epis.

Graham, fifth Earl and first Marquis of Montrose was born in 1612, probably either at Kincardine, or at Mugdock Castle near Glasgow, then the chief residences of the family. His mother was a daughter of the first Earl of Gowrie, the restless spirit who is remembered for his connection with the Raid of Ruthven. At the age of twelve, being, like Cromwell, the only son in a family of girls, Montrose, then Lord Graham, went to Glasgow with a tutor, worthy Master Forret, whose accurate account of every penny expended affords to the curious reader of the present day a perfect picture of the youthful cavalier and his establishment. Three years later, his father meanwhile having died, the young Earl passed to St. Andrews University. Here again his accounts show him leading a gay and generous life—playing at golf, shooting at the butts, where he won the silver arrow, playing chess and cards, entertaining his friends to supper, giving money to caddies, grooms, and beggars, helping a poor French student to the charges for his degree, and in leisure moments scribbling verses and conning his favourite books—the old romances of chivalry, and the lives of Sir Walter Raleigh, of Cæsar, and of Alexander.

Glasg. 1, 10, No. 5). Sir John the Graham, it will be remembered, took a leading part with Wallace in the Wars of Independence, and fell at Falkirk in 1298. Of the Marquis's immediate ancestors the first earl fell at Flodden, the second was killed at Pinkie, the third was Lord Treasurer, Chancellor, and Viceroy of Scotland. The fourth, the poet's father, carried the sword of state at the opening of the Scots Parliament in 1616, and is remembered for the duel he fought with Sir James Sandilands, in the High Street of Edinburgh, to avenge the murder of a kinsman.

The gallant young nobleman was a welcome guest at the mansions round St. Andrews, and in one of these, Kinnaird Castle, at the early age of seventeen, he wooed and married Lady Magdalene Carnegy, one of Lord Southesk's six daughters. By her he had three sons, one of whom succeeded him in the title.

Three years after his marriage, Montrose finished his education in the manner usual with young men of rank in Scotland at that time, by travel on the continent. He visited Rome, France, and the Low Countries, returning in 1636 to make his first appearance at the court of Charles I. At that period he is thus described by Thomas Sydney: "He was of a middle stature and most exquisitely proportioned limbs, his hair of a light chesnut, his complexion betwixt pale and ruddy, his eye most penetrating, though inclining to grey, his nose rather aquiline than otherwise. In riding the great horse and making use of his arms he came short of none. I never heard much of his delight in dancing, though his countenance and his other bodily endowments were equally fitting the court as the camp." A contemporary pamphlet, *Montrose Redevivus*, somewhat later describes him as "a man of a very princely courage and excellent addresses, which made him for the most part be used by all princes with extraordinary familiarity."

Scotland, just then, was approaching a great political crisis. James VI., after his accession to the English throne, had established Episcopacy in his northern kingdom, and Charles was pushing matters further.

In July, 1637, the attempt was made to introduce the
Liturgy, and the signal for resistance was given in St.
Giles's by Jenny Geddes with her flying stool and her
"Out, fause thief! Dost say mass at my lug?" In
1638 the nation, threatened with a religious tyranny,
to a man signed the National Covenant, swearing
solemnly to stand shoulder to shoulder in defence of
religious liberty. This bond was signed by Montrose,
and he was presently entrusted by the Committee of
Estates with a military commission against the Marquis of Huntly and the town of Aberdeen, both of
these being supporters of prelacy. In this undertaking he was entirely successful, routing the forces
of Huntly and sacking Aberdeen; and shortly afterwards, when the army of the Covenant, on its way to
England, came face to face with the army of the
king, Montrose was the first man to ford the Tweed
under the English fire.

About this period, however, the policy of the
Covenanting party in Scotland began to assume a
sinister aspect. At first the party had merely been
one for defence of the liberties of Scotland, but now,
like most popular factions when they attain to power,
it began to assume the offensive, and, in the interest
of particular tenets, to threaten even the existence of
the throne. This change was largely owing to the rise
to power of the dark, subtle, and ambitious Earl of
Argyle, a hereditary foe of the house of Graham.
Probably it did not need a personal motive just then
to induce the chivalrous Montrose to rally to the
Royalist side; the change of front of his party was

enough. At first he had taken up arms for justice to the people; now, when the crown itself appeared to be in danger, he took up arms for justice to the king. In suspicion of the motives of Argyle he had already drawn up a bond which was signed at Cumbernauld, Lord Wigton's seat, by nineteen noblemen, setting forth that, while they supported the Covenant, they also intended to maintain loyalty to the throne. On discovery of this bond, in May 1641, Montrose and certain others, including his sister's husband and his own close friend, Lord Napier, were thrown into Edinburgh castle, where they lay imprisoned for ten months.

This imprisonment identified Montrose with the Royalists, and when the Solemn League and Covenant of 1643, a much more aggressive document than the National Covenant of 1638, was signed in Scotland, he withheld his name, and appeared definitely in the opposite camp.

Charles had raised the royal standard at Nottingham in August, 1642, and throughout the following year his Cavaliers had proved at least equal to the forces of the English Parliament opposing them. But in 1644 a Scottish army crossed the Border, and in conjunction with the forces of the English Roundheads, inflicted on Charles the crushing defeat of Marston Moor. It was now, when the Royalist cause seemed almost desperate, that the genius of Montrose found its opportunity. Raised by Charles to the dignity of Marquis, and appointed the king's Lieutenant-General in Scotland, he made his way in disguise, through

Q   V difficulties and adventures which make the journey read like a romance, from Carlisle into the Highlands. He raised the king's standard suddenly in Athole, where he was joined by several of the clans and by a body of Irish sent over by the Earl of Antrim, and dashing forthwith upon the nearest Covenanting army, won his first victory for Charles at Tippermuir, and took Perth.

This was done on September 1, 1644, and his campaign during the next twelve months remains one of the most brilliant episodes in history. From point to point of the country he dashed, often with scant resources, sometimes with none; at each turn—at Aberdeen, Dundee, Aldearn, and Alford—striking some decisive blow; overthrowing, one after another, the generals of the estates; crushing the Clan Campbell at Inverlochy; and forcing his great enemy, Argyle himself, again and again to flee. Finally, by his victory over General Baillie at Kilsyth on August 15, 1645, he became master of Scotland.

Montrose was then at the summit of his fortunes. Appointed Captain-General and Lieutenant-Governor of Scotland, he held a court at Bothwell, and received congratulations and assurance of support from all who were favourable to the royal cause. The task which he had set himself was accomplished, Scotland was the king's, and the temper and tact of the letters still preserved, dated from "our Leaguer at Bothwell," show that Montrose was as fit to hold the helm of state as he had been to win the kingdom. He had still, however, to fill another rôle in history, and to

add to the renown of his military achievement and
of his courtly demeanour in the hour of triumph the
example of a heroic character in face of defeat,
disappointment, and death.

A month after his crowning victory at Kilsyth he
was endeavouring to effect a junction with the king's
forces in the north of England when, lying with a
small part of his following at Philiphaugh on the
Ettrick, he was surprised by a part of the Covenanting
army withdrawn from England under David Lesley,
and suffered a disastrous defeat. He himself, when
all was lost, cut his way with a few friends through
the enemy, and with difficulty escaped.

Notwithstanding this blow, Montrose might still,
with his indomitable courage and fertility of resourse,
have rallied the Scottish Royalists, and redeemed the
lost cause ; but the king was now in the hands of his
enemies, and anxious to make terms. He therefore
ordered his general to lay down arms, and at the
second message Montrose obeyed, taking care first to
stipulate for the lives and property of his friends.
Then, bidding those who had helped his cause a
regretful farewell, he retired to Holland.

He was at the Hague when the news reached him
of the execution of Charles, and so affected was he by
this, that it is said he fell down in a swoon. His
chaplain afterwards found on the floor of his room
the lines on the event beginning, "Great, Good, and
Just," which show the passionate intensity of his
feelings, and which appear to have become highly
popular among the Royalists. From that time the

Marquis did not cease to urge the young prince, now
Charles II., to make an effort to assert his rights, and
many of the letters are extant in which Charles I.'s
sister, the Queen of Bohemia, and other noble ladies,
with whom Montrose appears to have been in high
favour, endeavoured to encourage him and support
his scheme.

At last, in the spring of 1650, commissioned by the
king, and supported by some foreign troops and
treasure, he landed in Caithness and began his last campaign. The drama upon this occasion was short and
tragic. The country in which he had landed proved
hostile, and as the little army marched southward the
inhabitants held aloof. It was in vain that he used
every inducement, and displayed a special standard
which had been prepared to excite pity and indignation for the death of Charles I. The country would
not rise. His only hope was, as in 1644, to strike
some decisive blow; but he had now less trusty metal
to effect his purpose with. He was, however, pushing
forward with this intention when, at Invercarron, on
the confines of Ross-shire, he was surprised by Colonel
Strachan with a body of cavalry sent to scour the
country. The Royalist troops—German mercenaries
and Orkney fishermen—made hardly any resistance;
the greater number of the Cavaliers were either cut
down or taken prisoner; and Montrose himself, severely
wounded and his horse shot under him, was with
difficulty remounted and extricated from the pursuit.
After changing clothes with a Highland kern, and
wandering for several days in dire extremity, being

reduced, it is said, to eat his gloves, he was seized by
Macleod of Assynt. That chief, there is reason to
believe, had formerly served with Montrose, and the
marquis expected to find protection at his hands.
Assynt, however, delivered up Montrose to General
Lesley, and claimed and received for the transaction
the published reward of £1000, and four hundred
bolls of meal.*

Treated with every ignominy by his exultant enemies,
the captive Marquis was dragged from town to town
in the mean dress in which he had been taken. Once,
attired in female clothes, and helped by the Lady of
Grange, at whose husband's house in Fife he was
lodged, he had almost escaped, when the accident of
a drunken soldier betrayed him. Before he reached
Edinburgh he had been condemned to a barbarous
death, and when he arrived at the Water-gate in the
afternoon of a bleak day in May he found a cruel
pageant prepared for him. He was mounted high
and bareheaded upon a cart, while the hangman, clad
in the Montrose livery, rode before him covered. His
hands, by a refinement of cruelty, were tied, with the
idea, it is said, that if the populace stoned him he
should be defenceless. The rabble, however, struck
by his noble and stately bearing, wept and murmured
at his cruel fate. On the following Monday, in the
Parliament House, where he was brought to receive

---

* For the latest summing up of the evidence on this much-
debated point see the appendix to the new translation of Wishart's
Memoirs of Montrose, by Canon Murdoch and Mr. Morland
Simpson. London: Longmans, Green, & Co. 1893.

his sentence, every indignity and much vituperation
were heaped upon him.   He replied to his accusers
with a calm reason and eloquence which must have
made any less hardened than they to pause.   In
particular he pointed out that the deeds for which he
was arraigned had in every case been done under the
king's commission.   But his death had been resolved
upon, and he was forced unwillingly to kneel while
they read his sentence.   This was to the effect that
he should be hanged, drawn, and quartered, his head
fixed on the Tolbooth of Edinburgh, and his limbs
above the gates of the four chief cities.

This sentence was carried out on the Tuesday of
the following week.   On the night previous he had
written with a diamond on the window of his prison
the lines, " Let them bestow on every airth a limb,"
and he met his death with the high religious resigna-
tion which these lines express.   On the way to
execution, to which he was compelled to walk, he is
described as stepping "along the streets with so great
state, and there appeared in his countenance so much
beauty, majesty, and gravity as astonished the be-
holders ; and many of his enemies did acknowledge
him to be the bravest subject in the world, and in him
a gallantry that graced all the crowd --more beseeming
a monarch than a mere peer."   He was hanged on a
gallows thirty feet high, after presenting four pieces of
gold to the executioner, and making a speech which
ended with the words, " I leave my soul to God, my
service to my prince, my goodwill to my friends, my
love and charity to all."

Thus, on May 21, 1650, in the thirty-ninth year of his age, died Montrose, a nobleman whose bold genius and fiery energy won for him in a few short months the most brilliant reputation of his age, a hero who probably, as his contemporary, Cardinal de Retz, declared, comes nearest among moderns to the characters depicted by Plutarch. Eleven years later the whirligig of time brought its revenge. The head of Montrose was taken down from the Tolbooth, where it was presently replaced by that of his arch-enemy, Argyle. The body was exhumed and the remains were interred with national honours — mourning processions and salvoes of cannon—in the cathedral of St. Giles. The hero's heart, however, is not there. On the night of his execution some of his friends exhumed the body, and removed and em-balmed the heart. This, enclosed in a steel casket made from his sword, underwent in the hands of Montrose's relatives, Lord Napier's family, many romantic adventures in Holland, India, and France, till, in the troubles of the French Revolution, it was finally concealed or lost.

The *Memoirs of Montrose* (1639-1650) were first written by the Marquis's chaplain, George Wishart, afterwards Bishop of Edinburgh. The standard Life is that by Mark Napier, who also wrote a volume of "Memoirs" of his hero. More recently have appeared monographs by Mr. Mowbray Morris, and by Lady Violet Greville, herself a lineal descendant of the Grea Marquis. Of Montrose's poems, one at least, the epitaph on Charles I., was probably printed during its

author's lifetime.* Eight were printed in Watson's
Choice Collection of Scots Poems in 1711. The pieces
have been printed again among *Several Scots Poems*
(Edinburgh, 1745), and in Lady Violet Greville's
memoir, the latter volume containing two additional
compositions. The " Love Verses " were engraved in
Johnson's *Musical Museum* to the ancient tune of
"Chevy Chase." They also appear in Ritson's *Scottish
Song*, I. 59.

The poems of Montrose are exactly such as might
have been expected from a character like that of the
Marquis. Ardent and somewhat unequal, they are
the production of the man of action rather than the
man of letters, the work of one who cared more for
the thought than for its manner of expression, yet
whose thought is of itself so noble that in spite of all
shortcomings the verse lives and must always live in
the national mind and heart.

Of the stanzas entitled " Love Verses " it has been
supposed that the meaning does not lie quite on the
surface. They were written, it is believed, when
Montrose's wife was dead, and as, notwithstanding
his favour with the ladies of highest rank of his time,
he is not known to have loved again, the verses are
supposed to have a political signification, the speaker
being the king, and the mistress representing the
state. Whether or not this hypothesis be true, the
best stanzas of the poem remain among the best
stanzas of the cavalier poets. Montrose's other

* See Pepys' *Memoirs*, I. 9.

poems, all too few in number, may be left to explain
themselves. If here and there a line appear somewhat extravagant the reader may be asked to remember
that the poet was no mere maker of empty verse. In
the words of a recent critic, " Montrose's deeds had
given a solid foundation to his most swelling words ;
what would be ridiculous excess in a common man is
moderation in the mouth of the hero of Inverlochy
and Kilsyth."

LOVE VERSES. ·

FIRST PART

Y dear and only love, I pray
   That little world of thee
Be governed by no other sway,
   Than purest monarchy.
For if confusion have a part,
   Which virtuous souls abhor,
I'll call a synod in my heart,
   And never love thee more.

As Alexander I will reign,
   And I will reign alone;
My thoughts did evermore disdain
   A rival on my throne.
He either fears his fate too much,
   Or his deserts are small,
Who dares not put it to the touch,
   To gain or lose it all.

But I will reign and govern still,
   And always give the law,
And have each subject at my will,
   And all to stand in awe.

But 'gainst my batteries if I find,
　　Thou kick, or vex me sore,
As that thou set me up a blind,
　　I'll never love thee more.

And, in the empire of thine heart,
　　Where I should only be,
If others do pretend a part,
　　Or dare to vie with me.
Or if committees thou erect,
　　And go on such a score,
I'll laugh and sing at thy neglect,
　　And never love thee more.

But if thou wilt prove faithful then,
　　And constant to thy word,
I'll make thee glorious by my pen
　　And famous by my sword.
I'll serve thee in such noble ways
　　Was never heard before;
I'll crown and deck thee all with bays,
　　And love thee more and more.

SECOND PART.

My dear and only love, take heed
　　How thou thyself dispose:
Let not all longing lovers feed
　　Upon such looks as those.

I'll marble-wall thee round about,
　Myself shall be the door,
And if thy heart chance to slide out
　I'll never love thee more.

Let not their oaths, like volleys shot,
　Make any breach at all,
Nor smoothness of their language plot
　Which way to scale the wall,
Nor balls of wildfire love consume
　The shrine which I adore ;
For if such smoke about thee fume
　I'll never love thee more.

I know thy virtues be too strong
　To suffer by surprise ;
If that thou slight their love too long
　Their siege at last will rise,
And leave thee conqueror, in that wealth
　And state thou wast before :
But if thou turn a commonwealth,
　I'll never love thee more.

And if by fraud or by consent
　Thy heart to ruin come,
I'll sound the trumpet as I wont,
　Nor march by tuck of drum,
But hold my arms, like Achæus, up,
　Thy falsehood to deplore,
And bitterly will sigh and weep,
　And never love thee more.

I'll do with thee as Nero did
  When he set Rome on fire,
Not only all relief forbid,
  But to a hill retire,
And never shed a tear to save
  Thy spirit, grown so poor;
But laugh and smile thee to thy grave,
  And never love thee more.

Then shall thy heart be set by mine,
  But in far different case;
For mine was true, so was not thine,
  But looked like Janus' face.
For as the waves with every wind,
  So sails thou every shore,
And leaves thy constant heart behind—
  How can I have thee more?

My heart shall with thee sure be fixed,
  For constancy most strange;
And thine shall with the moon be mixed,
  Delighting aye in change.
Thy beauty shined at first so bright,
  And woe is me therefor,
That ever I found thy love so light
  That I could love no more.

Yet, for the love I bare thee once,
  Lest that thy name should die,
A monument of marble stone
  The truth shall testify;

That every pilgrim passing by
  May pity and deplore,
And, sighing, read the reason why
  I cannot love thee more.

The golden laws of love shall be
  Upon these pillars hung—
A single heart, a simple eye,
  A true and constant tongue.
Let no man for more love pretend
  Than he has hearts in store:
True love begun will never end;
  Love one, and love no more.

And when all gallants ride about
  More monuments to view,
Whereon is written, in and out,
  Thou traitorous and untrue;
Then, in a passion, they shall pause
  And thus say, sighing sore,
"Alas! he had too just a cause
  Never to love thee more."

And when that tracing goddess, Fame,
  From east to west shall flee,
She shall record it to thy shame,
  How thou hast lovèd me,
And how in odds our love was such
  As few have been before—
Thou lov'dst too many, I too much; .
  So I can love no more.

The misty mount, the smoking lake,
  The rock's resounding echo,
The whistling winds, the woods that shake
  Shall all with me sing heigho ;
The tossing seas, the tumbling boats,
  Tears dripping from each oar,
Shall tune with me those turtle notes
  I'll never love thee more.

As doth the turtle, chaste and true,
  Her fellow's death regret,
And daily mourns for her adieu,
  And ne'er renews her mate ;
So, though thy faith was never fast—
  Which grieves me wondrous sore—
Yet I shall live in love so chaste
  That I shall love no more.

LINES WRITTEN IN HIS COPY OF QUINTUS CURTIUS WHEN A YOUTH.

As Philip's noble son did still disdain
    All but the clear applause of merited fame,
And nothing harboured in that lofty brain
    But how to conquer an eternal name,
So great attempts, heroic ventures, shall
Advance my fortune, or renown my fall.

EPITAPH ON A DOG

*Belonging to the Marquis of Newcastle, fighting with
another, and killed in anger by Hamilton.*

HERE lies a dog whose quality did plead
Such fatal end from a renownèd blade :
And blame him not that he succumbèd now,
E'en Hercules could not combat against two.
For whilst he on his foe revenge did take
He manfully was killed behind his back.
Then say, to eternize the cur that's gone,
He fleshed the maiden sword of Hamilton.

R   V

IN PRAISE OF WOMEN.

WHEN Heaven's great Jove had made the world's
    round frame,
Earth, water, air, and fire, above the same,
The rolling orbs, the planets, spheres, and all
The lesser creatures in the earth's vast ball,
But, as a curious alchemist still draws
From grosser metals finer, and from those
Extracts another, and from that again   .
Another that doth far excel the same,
So framed he Man, of elements combined
To excel that substance whence he was refined.
But that pure creature, drawn from his breast,
Excelleth him as he excelled the rest,
Or as a stubborn stalk whereon there grows
A dainty lily or a fragrant rose:
The stalk may boast and set its virtues forth,
But, take away the flower, where is its worth?
But yet, fair ladies, you must know,
Howbeit I do adore you so,
Reciprocal your flowers must prove,
Or my ambition scorns to love.
A noble soul doth still abhor
To strike but where 'tis conqueror.

SOVEREIGNTY IN DANGER.

Can little beasts with lions roar,
And little birds with eagles soar?
Can shallow streams command the seas,
And little ants the humming-bees?
No, no, no, no—it is not meet
The head should stoop unto the feet.

ON THE FAITHLESSNESS AND VENALITY OF THE TIMES.

Unhappy is the man
  To whose breast is confined
The sorrows and distresses all
  Of an afflicted mind.

The extremity is great—
  He dies if he conceal,
The world's so void of secret friends,
  Betrayed if he reveal.

Then break, afflicted heart,
  And live not in these days,
When all prove merchants of their faith,
  None trusts what other says.

For when the sun doth shine
    Then shadows do appear,
But when the sun doth hide his face
    They with the sun retire.

Some friends as shadows are
    And fortune as the sun;
They never proffer any help
    Till fortune hath begun;

But if in any call
    Fortune shall first decay,
Then they, as shadows of the sun,
    With fortune run away.

SYMPATHY IN LOVE.

THERE'S nothing in this world can prove
So true and real pleasure
As perfect sympathy in love,
Which is a real treasure.

The purest strain of perfect love
In virtue's dye and season
Is that whose influence doth move,
And doth convince our reason.

Designs attend, desires give place,
Hope had, no more availeth ;
The cause removed, the effect doth cease,
Flame not maintained soon faileth.

The conquest then of richest hearts
Well lodged and trimmed by nature,
Is that which true content imparts—
When worth is joined with feature.

Filled with sweet hope then must I still
Love what's to be admired ;
When frowning aspects cross the will
Desires are more endeared.

Unhappy then, unhappy I,
　To joy in tragic pleasure,
And in so dear and desperate way
　To abound, yet have no treasure.

Yet will I not of Fate despair—
　Time oft in end relieveth—
But hope my star will change her air
　And joy where now she grieveth.

ON RECEIVING NEWS OF THE DEATH OF CHARLES I.

GREAT, Good, and Just, could I but rate
My grief with thy too rigid fate,
I'd weep the world in such a strain
As it should deluge once again.

But since thy loud-tongued blood demands supplies
More from Briareus' hands than Argus' eyes,
I'll sing thine obsequies with trumpet sounds
And write thine epitaph in blood and wounds.

ON THE DEATH OF CHARLES I.

BURST out my soul in main of tears,
  And thou, my heart, sigh's tempest move,
My tongue let never plaints forbear,
  But murmur still my crossèd love ;
Combine together all in one,
And thunder forth my tragic moan !

But tush, poor drop, cut breath, broke air !
  Can you my passions e'er express ?
No, rather but augment my care,
  In making them appear the less ;
Seeing that but from small woes words do come,
But great ones they are always dumb.

My swelling grief, then, bend yourself
  This fatal breast of mine to fill,
  The centre where all griefs distil ;
That, silent thus, in plaints I may
Consume and melt myself away.

Yet, that I may contented die,
  I only wish, before my death,
Transparent that my breast may be,
  Ere that I do expire my breath.
Since sighs, tears, plaints, express no smart,
It might be seen into, my heart.

WRITTEN ON THE EVE OF HIS EXECUTION.

Let them bestow on every airth a limb,
Then open all my veins that I may swim
To thee, my Maker, in that crimson lake;
Then place my parboiled head upon a stake,
Scatter my ashes, strew them in the air—
Lord! since thou knowest where all these atoms are,
I'm hopeful thou'lt recover once my dust,
And confident thou'lt raise me with the just.

THE
SEMPLES OF BELTREES

THE SEMPLES OF BELTREES.

THE poetical annals of Scotland in the troublous latter half of the seventeenth century are illuminated almost solely by the productions of a single family. These productions, moreover, differ from the work of the poets immediately preceding in the fact that they are written for the most part in the Scottish vernacular, and not in the fashionable English of the court.

Already the name of Semple had appeared among the "makars." In the previous century Robert Semple, whom some have confused with the Lord Semple of the time, had earned repute by writing a poem of considerable length entitled "The Sege of the Castel of Edinburgh," as well as a play, "The Regentis Tragedie," and several lighter productions.* But it is the work of the three Semples of the seventeenth century which has conferred a popular immortality upon the name.

* The "Sege" was printed by Lekprevik in 1573. Other of Semple's poems are contained in the Bannatyne MS. of 1568, printed by the Hunterian Club, and in *Scottish Poems of the Sixteenth Century.* "The Sempill Ballates, a series of Historical, Political, and Satirical Scottish Poems, ascribed to Robert Sempill, 1568-1583," was published at Edinburgh in 1872.

At the court of Queen Mary there was a young
gallant who owes a certain notoriety to a sentence of
John Knox—one of the pleasant things which that
Reformer was apt at saying about his contemporaries
of the opposite faction. "It wes weill knawin," he
writes, "that schame haistit mariage betwix John
Sempill, callit the Danser, and Marie Levingstoune,
surnameit the Lustie (fair)." This "Danser" was the
youngest son of Robert, third Lord Semple, of Castle
Semple in Renfrewshire, while Mary Livingston, one
of the "Queen's Maries," was a daughter of Alexander,
fifth Lord Livingston, the preceptor of the Queen.
Whether or not "schame haistit the mariage," as
Knox has so kindly recorded, Queen Mary appears
to have regarded it with great favour, dowering the
young couple with lands in Aberdeenshire, Ayrshire,
and Fife, while from Lord Semple they got Beltrees
and other property in Renfrewshire.

In the Beltrees papers it is stated that the son of
this gallant pair, afterwards Sir James Semple, "was
born about the year 1565, and being of an age with
King James VI., had his education with that learned
prince, with whom he became a most intimate com-
panion, and enjoyed some very honourable offices in
the state." The heir of Beltrees was in fact named
after the young king, who, though an infant, was his
godfather. Their tutor was the celebrated historian
and poet, George Buchanan, and it was probably to
him that the young courtier, like his royal master,
owed his taste for letters. Semple completed his
education at St. Andrews, and, his father having died

in 1579, he probably, after leaving the university,
spent much of his time at court. He was ambassador
at the English court in 1599, was knighted by James
in the following year, and in 1601 he appears as
ambassador to France.

When the king wrote his *Basilicon Doron*, Semple,
who acted as his amanuensis, showed the MS. in
process to his friend Andrew Melville, the famous
divine. With little scruple Melville took advantage
of this indulgence, and, having made notes of what
was intended to be only a private tract, laid the
matter before the presbyteries. For this violation of
good taste he was sent to the Tower, where curiously
he owed the mitigation of his imprisonment to the
intercession of the man to whose friendship he had
played false, the laird of Beltrees. A little later,
Melville, having gone to France, fell to loggerheads,
on the subject of Calvinism, with Tilenus, a fellow-
professor at Sedan. Here again Semple came to his
help, writing in his interest a Latin tract *Scoti* Τoυ
Τυχογτοs *Paraclesis contra Danielis Tileni Silesii
Parænesin.* Besides this polemic, which was composed
in 1622, Sir James wrote other two controversial
essays, *Cassandra Scoticana to Cassander Anglicanus*
in 1618, and *Sacrilege Sacredly Handled*, a tract
against Scaliger and Selden, in 1619. As Sheriff-
Substitute of Renfrewshire, he is believed to have
taken part in the reception of James VI. at Paisley
Abbey in 1617; and the oration then recited before
the king by "a prettie boy of 9 yeeres age " was
probably written by him. To these compositions and

his single poem, *The Packman's Paternoster, or A Picktooth for the Pope,* he owes his place in Scottish literature.

Semple in 1594 married Egidia, or Geillis Elphinston, a daughter of Elphinston of Blythswood, by whom he had two sons and four daughters. He died in February, 1626.

Robert Semple, eldest son and successor of Sir James, was probably born in 1595. He matriculated at the College of Glasgow in March, 1613, when his name appears as " Robertus Semple, hæres de Bultreis." Little is known of his life, except that in the great civil war he fought on the side of Charles I. as an officer in the royal army. The difficulties of the family seem to date from that time. During the struggle Robert Semple not only lost the Irish property of Carberry, which had been conferred on his father by King James, but was compelled also in 1649 to sell part of his estate, disposing of it to Captain George Montgomery for £3000. It is recorded that he took an active part in the Restoration, but it does not appear that he was in any way recompensed for his losses in the cause of loyalty. His death must have occurred before 1669, for in that year his son, as laird of Beltrees, effected an excambion of part of his park meadow. By his wife, Mary, a daughter of Sir Thomas Lyon of Auldbar, he left a son, Francis, and a daughter, Elizabeth, married to Sir George Maxwell of Newark.

Owing, perhaps, to the troubled state of the times in which he lived, Robert Semple has left only two

or three compositions to the world, the first being
an addition to his father's poem "The Packman's
Paternoster," and the second the famous popular
elegy on Habbie Simson, "The Piper of Kilbarchan."
An epitaph on Sanny Briggs, in the same vein and
stanza as "The Piper," has also been attributed
to him.

Third, and, by his work, best known of this descent,
was Francis Semple. He is chiefly famous as author
of the humorous song " Maggie Lauder," but he was
also author of other pieces of spirit, notably "She
rose and let me in," "Hallow Fair," "The Blythsome
Bridal," and "The Banishment of Poverty."

The date of his birth is unknown, but if a popular
tradition of the neighbourhood is to be trusted, it may
be approximately fixed. The story runs that one day,
when the boy was walking with his grandfather, the
old man said, "Thy faither is a poet—thou maun try
thy hand. We'se gang the length of Castle Semple,
then let me hear it." When the stipulated distance
had been covered the grandfather's ears were regaled
with the following sentiment :

> There livit three lairds into the west,
>   And their names were Beltrees ;
> An the deil wad tak' twa awa',
>   The third wad live at ease.

Sir James, it is said, "straikit the heid, but nippit
the lug" of the youthful rhymer. As the old knight
died in 1626, and his son Robert was then only thirty,
his grandson Francis was probably not more, and

could hardly be less than ten years old at the time, which would set his birth in the year 1616.

Francis Semple appears to have lived a somewhat reckless life, following at a distance the tone of the Merry Monarch's court. He did not marry till 1655, when he espoused his cousin, Jean Campbell, a daughter of Campbell of Ardkinglas. Before that event he probably went through the amorous adventure chronicled in his poem, "She rose and let me in." The editor of *Lyric Gems of Scotland* states that the song was written in 1650; and R. A. Smith in *The Scotish Minstrel*, a Paisley production, states that by tradition the scene of the amour was the old castle of Auchinames, to the south of Kilbarchan—a house belonging to the Crawford family, but demolished in the early years of this century. William Crawford of Auchinames, who died in 1695, had a daughter Ellen, who is believed to have been the heroine of the song. She was afterwards married to Patrick Edmonston of Newton, but bore him no children.

At the same period Semple was also probably inclined to mix as laird in such scenes of rural jollity as he has pictured in his "Hallow Fair" and his "Blythsome Bridal." In the *Paisley Repository*, and the Paisley *Annual Miscellany*, several traditions of the laird of Beltrees are recorded. Among other doings he appears to have furnished humorous epitaphs for several deceased characters of his neighbourhood. He also, when Glasgow lay under martial law during Cromwell's visitation, first outraged and then gained over the commanding officer by sending the required notification of his arrival in town in humorous rhyme.* The officers, it is said, became so enamoured of his company that they kept him in Glasgow two weeks longer than he had intended. There is a tradition also that the Semples introduced fox-hunting into Renfrewshire, and kept the first pack of foxhounds. Possibly the laird who effected this service was Francis Semple, and if so, this may be counted as one of the means by which he emptied his purse.

By his careless style of living Semple appears to have fallen into pecuniary difficulties. Hornings and arrests seem to have been common occurrences with him, and after his father's death he parted with his lands piece-meal. Nothing, however, could make him look sourly on life, and his "Banishment of Poverty" contains a lively account of one of his monetary distresses. He was helped out of the particular difficulty there described, he shows, by the kindness of James, Duke of Albany, afterwards James VII. Possibly that prince's assistance took the substantial shape of an appointment as Sheriff-Depute of Renfrewshire. At anyrate, Semple received that office before 1677.

Whatever was the royal favour, the laird of Beltrees repaid it by his loyalty. On one occasion, indeed, he nearly lost his life in the cause of order. It was the time of hill preachings or conventicles—of Drumclog and Bothwell Brig. A ringleader of the disorders was one Walter Scott, a late magistrate of Renfrew.

* See Stenhouse's note on "Maggie Lauder" in Johnson's *Museum.*

S   V

Semple, in pursuit of his duty as sheriff, arrested this man, and, a riot ensuing, the prisoner was rescued, and Beltrees beaten and wounded to the danger of his life.

Some of the poet's straits were the result of a habit of cautionry which at that time was sapping the foundations of society. From this and other causes Semple to the last appears to have been pressed for means. Perhaps his latest extant letter, dated in 1681, is one concerning money affairs. He was still, however, to judge from a sentence of the letter, able to entertain his kinsman, Lord Semple. He died, according to Law's *Memorials*, on March 12, 1682, leaving two sons, Robert and James.

The lands of Beltrees, or part of them, remained in the hands of the poet's descendants till 1758, when they were sold to M'Dowall of Castle Semple. Robert, the last of the race to be laird of Beltrees, died at Kilbarchan in 1789 at the age of 102.

The poetry of this poetical family is linked together in somewhat curious fashion, entailing the necessity of considering together the work of the three generations.

"The Packman's Paternoster," which bears on its title-page the curious invitation,

> This pious poeme buy and read,
> For off the Pope it knocks the head,

after being printed during the lifetime of its original author, Sir James Semple, was republished in 1669 with extensive additions by his son Robert, the parts belonging to each writer being quaintly marked by initials. The poem represents a debate between a pedlar and a priest regarding various doctrines of the Roman Church. The priest, being hard pressed in argument, refers the matter to the prior of a neighbouring convent. The prior, however, on hearing the case, treats both appellants as heretics, and proposes to lay them by the heels ; whereupon the packman turns and makes off, being by the way, however, relieved of his pack, which is seized by one of the friars. The whole forms a satire of considerable power and pungency, which must have been highly effective in its time, and which is still readable for its smoothness of versification and its salting of dry humour.

Robert Semple's "Piper of Kilbarchan," after appearing on various broadsides, was printed in Watson's *Choice Collection of Comic and Serious Scots Poems* in 1711. The hero of the piece was town piper of Kilbarchan, the neighbouring village to Beltrees, where his effigy, blowing the bags, still adorns the town steeple, and his tombstone is to be seen in the kirkyard. An account of him is furnished in the Paisley *Annual Miscellany* of 1612. Semple's poem is acknowledged by Allan Ramsay and Hamilton of Gilbertfield to be the first example of the felicitous stanza in which it is written. With the "Epitaph on Sanny Briggs" it keeps fresh the memory of Robert Semple as the author of a certain humorous Scottish vein in which he has been followed but hardly surpassed by later poets.

Of Francis Semple's poetry most is cast in the style and atmosphere of "Christ's Kirk on the Green." "Maggie Lauder," printed first by Herd, "Hallow Fair," taken by Maidment from a stall copy of 1790, and "The Blythsome Bridal," included by Watson in 1706, afford together a picture of the character, manners, and merriment of ancient Scottish rural life which, for humour, energy, and colour, was unsurpassed by anything in the popular literature of the country, excepting the compositions of James V., till Burns took up his pen. "She rose and let me in," carried to England by Cromwell's officers, and printed first with its tune in Playford's *Choice Ayres and Songs* in 1683, remains as excellent in another way. "Old Longsyne," printed first from the Beltrees papers in 1849, deals with a sentiment which exercised the pens of several Scottish poets before Burns trimmed it to the shape in which it is popular at present. If it appears somewhat unequal, the critic must at least admit that in the elder poet's production there are lines and epithets which are worthy of Burns himself.

The first and only collected edition of the poems of the Semples of Beltrees was edited by James Paterson, and published by T. G. Stevenson at Edinburgh in 1849. The volume, however, does not include "Hallow Fair," which is attributed to Francis Semple by the historian of Scottish poetry, Dr. Irving; and the editor has inserted a "Discourse between Law and Conscience," which is not the work of any of the lairds of Beltrees.

THE
PACKMAN'S PATERNOSTER.

A CONFERENCE BETWEEN A PEDLER AND A PRIEST.

 POLAND pedler went upon a day
Unto his parish priest to learn to pray:
The priest said, "Packman, thou must
haunt the closter
To learn the Ave and the Paternoster."

Packman.

Now, good Sir Priest, said he, what talk is that?
I hear you speak, but God in Heaven knows what.

Priest.

It is, said he, that holy Latin letter
That pleaseth God well, and our Lady better.

Packman.

Alas, Sir John,* I'll never understand them,
So must I leave your prayers as I fand them.

---

* Some priests were addressed with the title of " Sir," and
were known as the Pope's knights.

Priest.

Tush, tush, says he, if thou list to learn
The Latin prayers rightly to discern,
And sojourn but a little with me here,
Within a month I shall make thee parqueer.*

Packman.

Parqueer! said he; that will be but in saying;
In words, not sense, a prattling, not a praying.
Shall I, Sir John, a man of perfect age,
Pray like an idle parrot in a cage?

Priest.

A parrot can but prattle, for her part,
But towards God hath neither hand nor heart.

Packman.

And seeing I have head and heart to pray,
Should not my heart know what my tongue does say?
For when my tongue talks, if my heart miscarry,
How quickly may I mar your Ave Marie!
And I, Sir, having many things to seek,
How shall I speed, not knowing how I speak?

Priest.

Because that God all tongues doth understand,
Yea, knows the very thoughts before the hand.

* "By heart" (par cœur), or "by the book" (par quair).

Packman.

Then, if I think one thing and speak another,
I will both crab Christ and our Lady His Mother;
For when I pray for making up my pack, man,
Your Ave Marie is not worth a plack, man.

Priest.

Thy Latin prayers are but general heads,
Containing every special that thou needs :
The Latin serves us for a liturgy,
As medicines direct the chirurgy ;
And in this language mass is said and sung :
For private things pray in thy mother-tongue.

Packman.

Then must I have a tongue, Sir John, for either,
One for the Mother, another for the Father.

Priest.

Thinks thou the Mother does not know such small
    things ?
Christ is her Son, man, and He tells her all things.

Packman.

But, good Sir John, where learned our Lady her Latins,
For in her days were neither mass nor matins,
Nor yet one priest that Latin then did speak,
For holy words were then all Hebrew and Greek ?
She never was at Rome, nor kissed Pope's toe ;
How came she by the mass, then, would I know ?

Priest.

Packman, if thou believe the legendary,
The mass is elder far than Christ or Mary;
For all the patriarchs, both more and less,
And great Melchisedec himself said mass.

Packman.

But, good Sir John, spake all these fathers Latin?
And said they mass in surplices and satin?
Could they speak Latin long ere Latin grew?
And without Latin no mass can be true.
And as for heretics that now translate it,
False miscreants, they shame the mass, and slate it.

Priest.

Well, Packman, faith, thou art too curious,
Thy spur-blind zeal fervent but furious.
I'd rather teach a whole convene of monks
Than such a packman with his Puritan spunks.
This thou must know, that cannot be denied,
Rome reigned o'er all when Christ was crucified—
Rome ethnic then, but afterwards converted—
And grew so honest and so holy-hearted,
That now her emperor is turned in our pope,
His Holiness, as you have heard, I hope.
He made a law that all the world should pray
In Latin language to the Lord each day,
And thus in our traditions you may try,
Which, if you list to read, and shall espy
The Pope to be Christ's vicar, sole and sure,
And to the world's end so will endure.

Packman.

Surely this purpose puts me far aback,
And hath more points than pins in all my pack,
Whatever power you give to your Pope,
He may not make a man an ape, I hope.
But, good Sir John, before we farther go,
Resolve me this, since you assail me so :
How, when, and where this vicarage befell
Unto your Pope? I pray you briefly tell.

Priest.

Know you not? Peter when he went to Rome,
He then was execute, which was his doom,
And in his latter will and legacy
At Rome he left his full supremacy
Unto the Pope; which legacy was given
By Christ to Peter, when He went to heaven.
And so the Pope—though mediately, indeed,
By Peter—Christ's sole vicar doth succeed.
And every pope sensyne[1], from race to race,   [1] since then.
Succeeds each other in the papal place.

Packman.

By your assertion surely I perceive
You press to prove that Peter then did leave
Such legacy to those who did him murther.
Think ye such fond conceits your cause can further?

[The Packman proceeds to question the doctrines of purgatory,
transubstantiation, and the intercession of saints, and he satirizes
the institutions and abuses of the church—confession, indulgences,
the inquisition, and the venality of the clergy. Finally the
argument comes back to the question of language.]

Priest.

Now, Packman, I confess thou puts me to it;
But one thing I will tell thee if thou'lt do it—
Thou shalt come to our holy Prior, packman,
And he, perhaps, will buy all on thy back, man,
And teach thee better how to pray than any;
For such an holy man there are not many.
Be here to-morrow just 'tween six and seven,
And thou wilt find thyself halfway to heaven.

Packman.

Content, quoth I, but there is someting more
I must have your opinion in before,
In case the holy Prior have no leisure
To speak of every purpose at our pleasure.
There was but one tongue at the birth of Abel,
And many at the building up of Babel—
A wicked work which God would have confounded—
But when Christ came all tongues again resounded,
To build His Church by His apostles' teaching,
Why not in praying as well as in preaching?
Since prayer is the full and true perfection
Of holy service, saving your correction,
So if our Lord to mine own tongue be ready,
What need I then with Latin trouble our Lady?
Or if both these my prayer must be in,
I pray thee tell me at whom to begin.
And to pray jointly to them both as one,
Your Latin prayers then are quickly gone;
For Paternoster never will accord

With her, nor Ave Marie with our Lord.
If I get Him what need I seek another?
Or dare He do nothing without His Mother?
And this, Sir John, was once in question,
Disputed long with deep digestion—
Whether the Paternoster should be said
To God, or to our Lady, when they prayed,
When Master Mair,* of learned diversity,
Was Rector of our university,
They sate so long they cooled all their kail,
Until the master-cook heard of the tale,
Who like a madman ran among the clergy,
Crying, with many a *Domine me asperge*,
To give the Paternoster to the Father,
And to our Lady give the Aves rather;
And, like a Welshman, swore a great St. Davies,
She might content her well with creeds and aves;
And so the clergy, fearing more confusion,
Were all contented with the cook's conclusion.

Priest.

Packman, this tale is coined of the new.

Packman.

Sir John, I'll quit the pack if 't be not true.

  .   .   .   .   .   .

Last, since we say that God is good to speak to,
Who will both hear our text, and hear our eke too,

---

* John Mair, or Major, a well-known Scottish scholar, divine,
and historian, was born in 1469, and died in 1549.

What if He answer me in the Latin tongue
Wherein I pray and wherein mass is sung?
I must say, "Lord, I wot not what Thou sayest":
And he'll say, "Fool, thou wots not what thou
    prayest."
"Even, Lord," say I, "as good Sir John did teach
    me."
"Sir John!" saith he, "a priest unmeet to preach me;
Or in your mishent mouths once for to name me;
With different tongues and hearts, such Jock such
    Jamie.
For though I know more tongues than ye can tell,
False knaves, should ye not understand yoursel',
Gave I not you a tongue as well as heart,
inded. That both to Me should play an a-fold[1] part?
But like two double devils ye have dissembled."

At this Sir John he quakèd and he trembled
And said, "Good Packman, thou art so quick-witted,
Unto the Prior all must be remitted."
And so the Packman passed unto his lodging,
Having within his heart great grief and grudging.
Sometimes he doubted if the monks were men
Or monsters; for his life he could not ken.
He said Sir John was a fair fatted ox;
Sometimes he said he lookèd like John Knox;
But Knox was better versed into the Bible,
A study that Sir John held very idle.
They dive not deep into Divinity,
And trouble them little with the Trinity,
And are more learnèd in the legendary,

In lives of saints and of the Virgin Mary.
The only idol they embrace and kiss a
Is to prove servants unto Mistress *Missa.*

With such conceits the Packman passed the night,
With little sleep, until it was daylight ;
And by the peep of day he early rose,
And trimmed him finely in his holiday's hose,
And to Sir John's own chamber straight he went,
Who was attending.   So with one assent,
They hied them to the Prior both in haste,
To whom Sir John began to give a taste
Of all the questions that had passed amongst them.
He called them heretics both, and vowed to hang
      them.
With that the Packman hurled through the closter,
And there he met with an ill-favoured foster,
Who quickly twined[1] him and all on his back.   [1] parted.
And then he learned to pray, "Shame fall the pack,
For if they have not freed me of my sin,
They sent me lighter out than I came in!"
And still he cried, "Shame fall both monks and friars !
For I have lost my pack and learned no prayers.
So farewell Ave, Creed, and Paternoster !
I'll pray in my mother-tongue, and quit the closter."

THE LIFE AND DEATH OF THE PIPER OF KILBARCHAN,

OR

The Epitaph of Habbie Simson,
Who on his drone bore mony flags;
He made his cheeks as red as crimson,
And babbed when he blew his bags.

KILBARCHAN now may say alas!
For she hath lost her game and grace,
Both Trixie and the Maiden-Trace;*
      But what remead?
For no man can supply his place—
      Hab Simson's dead.

Now who shall play "The day it daws,"
Or "Hunt's up when the cock he craws?"
Or who can, for our kirktown cause,
      Stand us in stead?
On bagpipes now nobody blaws,
      Sin' Habbie's dead.

---

* It was formerly the custom in Kilbarchan for the piper to
play a march called the Maiden-trace before the bride as,
previous to her marriage, she walked with her maidens three
times round the church.   "Hey trix, trim go trix" was a popular
song.   Irving prints it in his *History of Scottish Poetry.*

Or wha will cause our shearers shear¹?   ¹ mow.
Wha will bend up the brags o' weir²,   ² strike up the
                                               war-notes.
Bring in the bells, or good play meir
      In time of need?
Hab Simson could, what needs you speir³?   3 inquire.
      But now he's dead.

So kindly to his neighbours neist,
At Beltane and Saint Barchan's feast
He blew, and then held up his breast,
      As he were weid⁴;   4 wod, wild.
But now we need not him arrest,
      For Habbie's dead.

At fairs he played before the spearmen⁵,   5 provost's gua
All gaily graithed⁶ in their gear, men,   6 clad.
Steel bonnets, jacks, and swords so clear then,
      Like any bead.
Now wha will play before such weir-men⁷,   7 warriors.
      Sin Habbie's dead?

At clerk-plays⁸, when he wont to come,   8 stage plays.
His pipe played trimly to the drum,
Like bykes of bees he gart it bum,
      And tuned his reed:
Now all our pipers may sing dumb
      Sin' Habbie's dead.

And at horse races many a day
Before the black, the brown, the grey,*
He gart his pipe, when he did play.
  Baith skirl and screed ;
Now all such pastime's quite away
  Sin' Habbie's dead.

picked.

He counted was a waled¹ wight-man,
And fiercely at football he ran ;

superiority.

At every game the gree² he wan
  For pith and speed ;
The like of Habbie wasna then.
  But now he's dead.

And then, besides his valiant acts,
At bridals he wan many placks,
He bobbit aye behind folks' backs,
  And shook his head :

jests.

Now we want many merry cracks³,
  Sin' Habbie's dead.

He was convoyer of the bride.

His dirk, named
after Montrose's
lieutenant.

With Kittock⁴ hinging at his side ;
About the kirk he thought a pride
  The ring to lead :

without.

But now we may gae but⁵ a guide,
  For Habbie's dead.

----

* The winning horse was led round in triumph after the race,
the piper playing before it.

So well's he keepit his decorum
And all the stots[1] of "Whipmegmorum,"   [1] steps of the dance.
He slew a man, and wae's me for him,
  And bore the feid[2];   [2] feud.
But yet the man wan hame before him,
  And was not dead.*

And when he played, the lasses leugh[3]   [3] laughed.
To see him teethless, auld, and teugh;
He wan his pipes beside Barcleugh †
  Withouten dread;
Which after wan him gear eneugh;
  But now he's dead.

Aye when he played, the gaislings gethered,
And when he spake the carl blethered,
On Sabbath days his cap was feathered,
  A seemly weed;
In the kirkyard his mare stood tethered
  Where he lies dead.

* The story is told that Habbie was playing his new tune of
"Whipmegmorum" when a tipsy villager thrust a knife into the
pipe-bag, and let out the wind. The piper, in sudden wrath at
the insult, drew his "kittock" and drove it at his assailant,
who fell to the ground. Habbie fled, and lay for a day in
hiding, thinking his man dead, before he discovered that in
seizing his knife he had drawn out only the handle, the blade
having remained in its sheath.

† With his wage as a herd boy.

T   V

Alas, for him my heart is sair,
For of his springs I gat a scare
At every play, race, feast, and fair,
But guile or greed;
We need not look for piping mair
Sin' Habbie's dead.

HALLOW FAIR.*

THERE'S mony braw Jockies and Jennies
Comes weel buskit into the fair,
Wi' ribbons on their cockernonies[1],   [1] snooded knots of hair.
And fouth[2] o' braw flour i' their hair.   [2] plenty.
Maggie sae brawly was buskit[3]   [3] dressed.
When Jockie was tied to his bride ;
The pownie was ne'er better whiskit
Wi' a cudgel that hung by his side.
     Sing fal de ral, la de.

But Willie, the muirland laddie,
Was mounted upon a gray cowt,
Wi' his sword by his side like a caddie,
To ca' in the sheep and the nowt[4].   [4] cattle.
Sae nicely his doublets did fit him,
They scarcely came down to mid-thie,
Wi' weel-powdered hair, hat, and feather,
Wi' houzen, curple, and tie[5].   [5] housing, crupper, and bridle-fastening.
     Sing fal de ral, la de.

* This gathering was held on All Saints Day in November. "Hallow Fair," says Maidment (*Scotish Ballads and Songs*, 1859), "which is now peculiar to the metropolis, was held on the Calton Hill some fifty years ago. The little boys used to arm themselves with whips, and accompany the cattle to their place of destination in their passage through the city."

But Maggie grew wondrous jealous
   To see Willie buskit sae braw,
And Wattie he sat i' the ale-house
   And hard at the bicker[1] did ca'.
Sae nicely as Maggie sat by him,
   He took the pint-stoup in his arms,
Quo' he, "I think they're right saucy
   That lo'es na good father's bairns."
      Sing fal de ral, la de.

But now it grew late i' the e'ening,
   And buchting[2] time was drawing near ;
The lasses had stanched a' their greening[3]
   Wi' fouth o' braw apples and pears.
There's Tibbie, and Sibbie, and Lily,
   Wha weel on the spindle can spin,
Stood glow'ring at signs and glass winnocks[4],
   But fient a ane[5] bade them come in.
      Sing fal de ral, la de.

"Gosh guide's! did ye e'er see the like o't?
   See, yonder's a bonnie black swan ;
It looks as it fain wad be at us—
   What's yon that it has in its han'?"
"Awa', daft gowk!" quo' Wattie,
   "It's nane but a rickle o' sticks ;
See, there's the deil and Bell Hawkie,
   And yonder's Mess James and Auld Nick.
      Sing fal de ral, la de.

But Bruckie played "Boo!" to Bawsie,
  And aff gaed the cowt like the win';
Puir Willie, he fell i' the causey,
  And bruized a' the banes in his skin;
The pistols fell out o' the hulsters,
  And were a' bedaubit wi' dirt;
The folks ran about him in clusters,
  Some leugh and said, "Lad, are ye hurt?"
      Sing fal de ral, la de.

The cowt wad let naebody near him—
  He was aye sae wanton and skeigh[1]—
The pedlar stan's he lap ower them,
  And gart a' the folk stan' abeigh[2]:
Wi' a' sneering behin' and before him,
  For sic is the mettle o' brutes,
Puir Wattie, and wae's me for him,
  Was forced to gang hame in his boots.
      Sing fal de ral, la de.

[1] shy, easily alarmed.

[2] aside.

MAGGIE LAUDER.

Wha wadna be in love
 Wi' bonnie Maggie Lauder?
A piper met her gaun to Fife
 And spiered what was't they ca'd her;
Richt scornfully she answered him,
 "Begone, you hallan-shaker[1]!
Jog on your gate[2], you bladderskate[3]!
 My name is Maggie Lauder."

"Maggie!" quoth he, "and, by my bags,
 I'm fidgin' fain to see thee:
Sit down by me, my bonnie bird;
 In troth I winna steer thee,
For I'm a piper to my trade,
 My name is Rob the Ranter;
The lasses loup as they were daft
 When I blaw up my chanter."

"Piper," quo' Meg, "hae ye your bags,
 Or is your drone in order?
If ye be Rob, I've heard o' you;
 Live you upo' the Border?

The lasses a' baith far and near,
    Have heard o' Rob the Ranter,
I'll shake my foot wi' richt gude will
    Gif ye'll blaw up your chanter."

Then to his bags he flew wi' speed;
    About the drone he twisted;
Meg up and walloped ower the green,
    For brawly could she frisk it.
"Weel done!" quo' he. "Play up!" quo' she.
    "Weel bobbed!" quo' Rob the Ranter,
"It's worth my while to play, indeed,
    When I hae sic a dancer!"

"Weel hae you played your part," quo' Meg;
    "Your cheeks are like the crimson:
There's nane in Scotland plays sae weel
    Sin' we lost Habbie Simson.
I've lived in Fife, baith maid and wife,
    This ten years and a quarter;
Gin ye should come to Anster Fair,*
    Speir ye for Maggie Lauder."

* Before the Union, Anstruther lint fair was a great gathering,
attended by merchants from all the northern countries of Europe.
The doings at it have been celebrated in Tennant's well-known
poem of "Anster Fair."

THE BLYTHSOME BRIDAL.

Fy, let us all to the bridal,*
[1] singing.　　　　For there will be lilting[1] there,
For Jockie's to be married to Maggie,
　　The lass wi' the gowden hair.
And there will be lang-kail and pottage
　　And bannocks of barley-meal,
And there will be good salt herring,
　　To relish a cog of good ale.
　　　　Fy, let us all to the bridal,
　　　　　　For there will be lilting there,
　　　　　　For Jockie's to be married to Maggie,
　　　　　　　　The lass wi' the gowden hair.

[2] shoemaker.　　And there will be Sandy the souter[2],
　　　　　　And Willie wi' the meikle mou';
[3] puddler.　　And there will be Tom the plouter[3],
　　　　　　And Andrew the tinkler, I trow;
And there will be bow-legged Robbie,
　　And thumbless Katie's good-man,
And there will be blue-cheeked Dallie,
　　And Laurie the laird o' the lan'.
　　　　Fy, let us all, &c.

* "The license of a Scottish bridal," says Allan Cunningham,
"if we may believe the northern painters and poets, was very
great. The riding for the bruse, the bedding, the stocking-
throwing, the eating, the dancing, and the drinking, would
require a volume."

And there will be sow-libber[1] Patey,
And plouky-faced[2] Wat i' the mill,
Capper-nosed[3] Gibbie, and Francie
That wins in the how[4] o' the hill.
And there will be Alaster Dougal,
That splee-footed Bessie did woo,
And sniffling Lily and Tibbie,
And Kirsty, that belly-god sow,
    Fy, let us all, &c.

[1] sow-gelder.
[2] pimply-faced.
[3] hook-nosed.
[4] lives in the hollow.

And Crampie, that married Steenie,
And coft[5] him breeks to his ——
And afterwards hanged for stealing,
Great mercy it happened no worse.
And there will be fairntickled[6] Hugh,
And Bess wi' the lily-white leg,
That gat to the south for breeding[7],
And banged up her wame in Mons Meg.
    Fy, let us all, &c.

[5] bought.
[6] freckled.
[7] manners.

And there will be Geordie M'Cowrie,
And blinking daft Barb'ra, and Meg,
And there will be blenched[8] Gillie-Whimple,
And peuter-faced, flichting[9] Joug.
And there will be happer-a—d[10] Nancy,
And fairy-faced Jeanie by name,
Glie'd[11] Katie, and fat-lugged Lizzie,
The lass wi' the gowden wame.
    Fy, let us all, &c.

[8] pale.
[9] anxious-faced, scolding.
[10] shrunk about the hips.
[11] squint-eyed.

[1] ill-humoured.

[2] giddy.

[3] scolding.

And there will be girn-again[1] Gibbie,
And his glaikit[2] wife, Jeanie Bell,
And measly-chinned flyting[3] Geordie,
The lad that was skipper himsel'.
There'll be all the lads and the lasses,
Set down in the midst o' the ha',

[4] onions, radishes, and broiled peas.

Wi' siboes and rifarts and carlings[4],
That are both sodden and raw.
Fy, let us all, &c.

[5] colewort, sweets, and thick gruel.
[6] mouthfuls.
[7] sheep's head broth, meal and water, and curd.
[8] crabs and shell-fish.
[9] dried haddocks.

There will be tartan, dragen, and bracken[5],
And fouth of good gappocks[6] of skate,
Pow-sodie, and drammock, and crowdie[7],
And caller nowt-feet in a plate.
And there will be partans and buckies[8],
Speldens[9], and haddocks eneugh,
And singed sheeps' heads, and a haggis,

[10] fat broth.

And scadlips[10] to sup till ye're fu'.
Fy, let us all, &c.

[11] curded-milk cheeses.
[12] thick cakes.
[13] new ale.

There will be good lappered-milk kebbocks[11],
And sowens, and farles, and baps[12],
And swats[13], and scrapit paunches,
And brandy in stoups and in caps.

[14] meal-broth and cabbage-stalks.
[15] drink.
[16] belch.
[17] grid.
[18] flounders.

And there will be meal-kail and custocks[14],
And skink[15] to sup till you rive[16],
And roasts, to roast on a brander[17],
Of flukes[18] that were taken alive.
Fy, let us all, &c.

Scraped haddocks, whelks, dulse, and tangle,
And a mill of good sneezin' to pree[1];   [1] horn of good
                                              snuff to try.
When weary with eating and drinking,
We'll rise up and dance till we dee.
Fy, let us all to the bridal,
For there will be lilting there,
For Jockie's to be married to Maggie,
The lass wi' the gowden hair.

THE
BANISHMENT OF POVERTY.*

Pox fa' that poltroon Poverty!
[1] Sad was.   Wae worth[1] the time that I him saw!
Sin' first he laid his fang on me
[2] could.   Myself from him I dought[2] ne'er draw.

His wink to me has been a law,
[3] dog that follows closely.   He haunts me like a penny-dog[3];
Of him I stand far greater awe
Than pupil does of pedagogue.

The first time that he met with me
Was at a clachan in the west;
Its name, I trow, Kilbarchan be,
Where Habbie's drones blew mony a blast.

[4] fortune.   There we shook hands—cauld be his cast[4]!
[5] low fellow.   An ill death may that custron[5] dee!
For then he grippit me full fast
When first I fell in cautionry.

---

* The full title of this piece was "The Banishment of Poverty,
by His Royal Highness J. D. A. (James Duke of Albany). To
the tune of 'The Last Good-night.'"

Yet I had hopes to be relieved,
  And freed from that foul lairdly loun,
Fernyear[1], when Whigs were ill mischieved,   [1] Last year.
  And forced to fling their weapons doun.

When we chased them from Glasgow toun,
  I with that swinger thought to grapple;
But when indemnity came doun
  The laidron[2] pu'd me by the thrapple[3].   [2] lazy knave.
                                                  [3] throat.

But yet, in hopes of some relief,
  A raid I made to Arinfrew,
Where they did bravely buff my beef,
  And made my body black and blue.

At Justice court I them pursue,
  Expecting help by their reproof;
Indemnity thought nothing due—
  The deil a farthing for my loof[4].   [4] palm.

But, wishing that I might ride east—
  To trot on foot I soon would tire—
My page allowed me not a beast;
  I wanted gilt to pay the hire.

He and I lap ower mony a syre[5],   [5] ditch.
  I heukit him at Calder-cult;
But lang ere I wan to Snipes-mire
  The ragged rogue took me a-whilt[6].   [6] in a state of
                                                  perturbation.

By Hollin-bush and Brig o' Bonnie

[1] moved quickly.

[2] cheats.

By Hollin-bush and Brig o' Bonnie
    We bickered[1] down towards Bankier;
We feared no reivers for our money,
    Nor whilly-whaes[2] to grip our gear.

My tattered tutor took no fear,
    Though we did travel in the mirk,
But thought it fit, when we drew near,
    To filch a forage at Falkirk.

No man would open me the door,
    Because my comrade stood me by;
They dread full ill I was right poor

[3] neglected.

    By my forecasten[3] company.

But Cunningham soon me espied;
    By hue and hair he brought me in,
And swore we should not part so dry,
    Though I were naked to the skin.

We bade all night, but lang ere day
    My curst companion made me rise;
I start up soon and took my way:
    He needed not to bid me twice.

But what to do we did advise;
    In Lithgow we might not sit down:
On a Scots groat we baited thrice,
    And in at night to Edinburgh town.

We held the Lang-gate¹ to Leith Wynd,   ¹ now Princes
 Where poorest purses use to be;   Street.
And in the Calton lodgèd syne,
 Fit quarters for such company.

Yet I the High-town fain would see,
 But that my comrade did me discharge;
He willed me Blackburn's² ale to pree, ² a celebrated
 And muff my beard that was right large. brewer of ale
               of the time.

The morn I ventured up the Wynd,
 And slunk in at the Netherbow,
Thinking that troker for to tyne³,   ³ lose.
 Who does me damage what he dow⁴.   ⁴ can.

His company he doth bestow
 On me, to my great grief and pain;
Ere I the thrang could wrestle through
 The loun was at my heels again.

I greined⁵ to gang on the plain-stanes, ⁵ longed.
 To see if comrades wad me ken:
We twa gaed pacing there our lanes,
 The hungry hour 'twixt twelve and ane.

Then I kenned no way how to fen⁶;   ⁶ make shift.
 My guts rumbled like a hurl-barrow⁷— ⁷ wheel-barrow.
I dined with saints and noblemen,
 Even sweet Giles and Earl of Murray.*

* *i.e.*, spent the dinner hour walking in St. Giles' Cathedral.

1 dog's testament,
i.e., there
would be
nothing left.

Tyke's test'ment[1] take him for their treat!
I needed not my teeth to pyke;
Though I was in a cruel sweat
He set not by, say what I like.

I called him Turk and traikit tyke[2],
And wearied him with many a curse:
My banes were hard like a stone dyke
No *Reg. Marie* was in my purse.

Kind Widow Caddel sent for me
To dine, as she had oft, forsooth:
But ah! alas, that might not be,
Her house was o'er near the Tolbooth.

.

Yet God reward her for her love
        And kindness, which I feetlie[3] fand
Most ready still for my behoof
        Ere this hell's hound took me in hand.

I slipped my page, and stoured[4] to Leith,
        To try my credit at the wine;
But foul a dribble filed[5] my teeth,
        He gripped me at the coffee sign.

I staw[6] down through the Nether-wynd,
        My Lady Semple's house was near;
To enter there was my design,
        When Poverty durst ne'er appear.

I dinèd there, but bade not lang.
  My Lady fain wad shelter me,
But oh! alas, I needs must gang,
  And leave that comely company.

Her lad convoyed me with her key
  Out through the garden to the fields;
Ere I the Links could graithly[1] see   [1] comfortably.
  My governor was at my heels.

I dought[2] not dance to pipe nor harp,   [2] could.
  I had no stock for cards and dice:
But I fure[3] to Sir William Sharpe,*   [3] fared, went.
  Who never made his counsel nice.

That little man he is right wise,
  And sharp as any brier can be;
He bravely gave me his advice
  How I might poison Poverty.

Quoth he, "There grows hard by the dial,
  In Hatton's garden, bright and sheen,
A sovereign herb called Pennyroyal,
  Whilk all the year grows fresh and green.

"Could ye but gather it fair and clean,
  Your business would go the better;
But let account of it be seen
  To the physicians of exchequer.

* Brother of Archbishop Sharpe, he was in succession Cashier
to the Treasury and Master of the Mint.
  U   V

"Or if that ticket ye bring with you,
  Come unto me, ye need not fear,
For I some of that herb can give you,
  Whilk I have planted this same year.

"Your page it will cause disappear,
  Who waits on you against your will;
To gather it I shall you lear
  In my own yards of Stoneyhill." *

But when I dread that would not work,
  I overthought me of a wile,
How I might at my leisure lurk,
  My graceless guardian to beguile.

It's but my galloping a mile
  Through Canongate, with little loss,
Till I have sanctuary a while
  Within the girth of Abbey-close.†

There I wan in, and blyth was I
  When to the inner court I drew;
My governor I did defy,
  For joy I clapt my wings and crew.

* Near Musselburgh.
† Even so late as the middle of the present century the precincts of Holyrood were a sanctuary for debtors. The boundary
is still marked by a stone in the street; beyond that the debtor
was safe from arrest.

There messengers dare not pursue,
  Nor with their wands men's shoulders steer ;
There dwell distressèd lairds eneugh,
  In peace, though they have little gear.

There twa hours I did not tarry
  Till my blest fortune was to see
A sight, sure by the mights of Mary,
  Of that brave Duke of Albany.

Where one blink of his princely eye
  Put that foul foundling to the flight ;
Frae me he banished Poverty,
  And gart him take his last good-night.

SHE ROSE AND LET ME IN.

THE night her sable mantle wore,
  And gloomy were the skies,
Of glittering stars appeared no more
  Than those in Nelly's eyes.
When at her father's yett I knocked,
  When I had often been,
She, shrouded only in her smock,
  Arose and let me in.

Fast locked within her close embrace,
  She trembling stood, ashamed;
Her swelling breast and glowing face
  And every touch inflamed.
My eager passion I obeyed,
  Resolved the fort to win,
And her fond heart was soon betrayed
  To yield and let me in.

Then, then, beyond expressing,
  Transporting was the joy,
I knew no greater blessing,
  So blest a man was I;
And she, all ravished with delight,
  Bid me oft come again,
And kindly vowed that every night
  She'd rise and let me in.

*   *   *   *   *   *

OLD LONGSYNE.

FIRST PART.

SHOULD old acquaintance be forgot,
  And never thought upon,
The flames of love extinguished
  And freely past and gone?
Is thy kind heart now grown so cold,
  In that loving breast of thine,
That thou canst never once reflect
  On old longsyne?

Where are thy protestations,
  Thy vows and oaths, my dear,
Thou mad'st to me, and I to thee,
  In register yet clear?
Is faith and truth so violate
  Unto the God divine,
That thou canst never once reflect
  On old longsyne?

Is't Cupid's fears, or frosty cares,
  That makes thy spirits decay:
Or is't some object of more worth
  That's stole thy heart away;

Or some desert makes thee neglect
   Him so much once was thine,
That thou canst never once reflect
   On old longsyne?

Is't worldly cares so desperate
   That makes thee to despair?
Is't that makes thee exasperate,
   And bids thee to forbear?
If thou of that were free as I,
   Thou surely should be mine;
If this were true we should renew
   Kind old longsyne.

But since that nothing can prevail,
   And all my hope is vain,
From these rejected eyes of mine
   Still showers of tears shall rain:
And though thou hast me now forgot,
   Yet I'll continue thine,
And ne'er forget for to reflect
   On old longsyne.

If e'er I have a house, my dear,
   That's truly callèd mine,
And can afford but country cheer,
   Or aught that's good therein;

Though thou wert rebel to the king,
  And beat with wind and rain,
Assure thyself of welcome, love,
  For old longsyne.

SECOND PART.

My soul is ravished with delight
  When you I think upon;
All griefs and sorrows take the flight
  And hastily are gone.
The fair resemblance of your face
  So fills this breast of mine,
No fate nor force can it displace,
  For old longsyne.

Since thoughts of you do banish grief,
  When I'm from you removed,
And if in them I find relief
  When with sad cares I'm moved,
How doth your presence me affect
  With ecstacy divine,
Especially when I reflect
  On old longsyne.

Since thou hast robbed me of my heart
  By those resistless powers
Which Madam Nature doth impart
  To those fair eyes of yours,

With honour it doth not consist
   To hold a slave in pine;
Pray let your rigour then desist,
   For old longsyne.

'Tis not my freedom I do crave
   By deprecating pains;
Sure, liberty he would not have
   Who glories in his chains;
But this—I wish the gods would move
   That noble soul of thine
To pity, since thou cannot love,
   For old longsyne.

William Hodge & Co., Printers, Glasgow.